TH

After Hardy's death a meeting was convened in Dorchester to discuss the question of a memorial to him . . . Asked my views on the matter, I recommended a statue of one of Hardy's best-known and most popular characters, with a medallion of Hardy himself on the plinth, to be erected on some elevated site on Egdon Heath, or the moorland so named in the novels. Hardy himself was, physically, not of monumental build, though he had a fine head. The figure I suggested was that of Tess of the D'Urbervilles as most suitable to the purpose, . . . anyhow my project was turned down, and Tess rejected in favour of the depressing object we now see at the top of the High Street, Dorchester.

Augustus John: CHIAROSCURO

THOMAS HARDY

a pictorial guide

Hugh Brasnett

with photographs by the author
and maps by Jenny Brasnett

LODGE
COPSE
PRESS

FOR JENNIFER

First Published by John Waite 1984
Second Edition Lodge Copse Press 1990

ISBN 0 9515609 0 5

Printed and bound by
Pardy Printers Ltd., Ringwood, Hampshire

Lodge Copse Press, 18 Lodge Road, Holt,
Wimborne, Dorset BH21 7DN

Front Cover: Faringdon Ruin, Winterborne Came.

CONTENTS

INTRODUCTION

I was born and grew up on the border of what has come to be known as the 'Hardy Country'. On Sunday jaunts into this literary landscape my father, hoping no doubt to kindle in his young sons' minds an interest in the writer (we had the Wessex novels at home, but *Chums Annual* and the daily adventures of Rupert Bear provided us with an adequate supply of fiction) would often point out to my brother and me places Hardy had used in his stories and novels. But father's imparted knowledge was indifferently received. Thomas Hardy remained to us a wizened-up old man, long since dead, whose maroon, morocco-bound books with their gilt-lettered spines were never lifted down from the book-shelves. What could an old man like that possibly have to say to young boys whose main interests in the landscape were the exploration of its hedgerows, swinging on gates, leaping (and frequently landing in) its many brooks and streams?

So it was that I was well into my thirties, had travelled the world and lived in many other parts, before on returning to Bournemouth I came to grips with this author I had so long neglected. And of course I was delightedly surprised. Here was no dry and dreary writer as I had imagined, but a poet and painter – a landscape painter who could sketch with a few swift phrases the inherent wonder and beauty of a scene, capturing the capricious moods of the weather, conversant with the wild and domesticated creatures living there and faithfully imparting that knowledge to the reader. Here was a writer who knew his people as fully as he knew his countryside, who could share their joys and sorrows, was proud of their independent ways and customs and their strength in the face of adversity. A man with a great sense of humour chuckling at the antics and oddities of his country folk, he was also a master ironist quick to seize on the foibles of those who took themselves too seriously. And, above all, he was a writer who looked on and wrote in anger about injustices, both of the gods and of mortal men. From his first unpublished book *The Poor Man and the Lady* to his final furore-raising novel *Jude the Obscure*, his pen as lance was frequently used to make significant thrusts at targets ranging from the humbug surrounding theological doctrine to *the aristocratic principle of blood before everything*. Hardy, I realised as I read him in his entirety, was a writer I had been foolish to ignore for so long.

When, however, I spoke to friends and acquaintances about my belated discovery I found that only too often they also shared my former ignorance. They had in many instances been put off by what they had heard or read about Thomas Hardy (he was dark, pessimistic, etc.), or, occasionally as in my own case, attempts had been made to interest them in the writer at a too early age. Schools had played their part by including his novels in the Eng. Lit. curriculum – how many worthy writers I wonder have been lost to us for years, often a lifetime, by such premature priming? – and Hardy is undoubtedly an author whose work is best not approached until one has experienced a wider measure of the world and the buffetings of fate than is usually acquired in the protected years of growing up. So I set about redressing the balance, and the book that follows is a penitent native son's unashamedly biased homage to the often misunderstood and sadly ignored genius of the Wessex bard.

Augustus John's characteristically dismissive comment on the Thomas Hardy memorial quoted at the front provides the keynote to the book. John, of course, was not the only one of Hardy's many friends and admirers to be affronted by such an essentially unHardyesque tribute to the writer. Sir Frederick Treves, who died a few years before Hardy, was nevertheless allowed a typically astringent aside by the editors who revised his memorable guide to the county, *Highways and Byways in Dorset*. Noting that Hardy is portrayed in knickerbockers with his feet resting upon a heap of horticultural specimens, Treves comments from beyond the grave: 'Criticism must be respectfully withheld, as it doubtless pleased the committee and subscribers who were responsible for its erection.'

However, returning to the distinguished and joyously forthright painter's quotation and its significance in relation to this photographic study, his alternative suggestion of a monumental Tess set in mid-stride somewhere in the heart of Egdon Heath might or might not have been a better way to honour the writer. Personally I have a horror of bronze or stone replicas, whether of persons once living or of characters they have created. By the very nature of their stony or verdigris immobility they mock the intentions of those who set them up and only the perching pigeons benefit. But it is, I feel, in his suggestion of the locale for such a memorial, 'Egdon Heath, or the moorland so named in the novels,' that John has grasped the nettle firmly by the stem. For, as I returned to explore the 'Hardy Country' anew, this time with his novels, stories and poems freshly in my mind, I could not help realising that the finest tribute to this writer was still to be found in the scenery and places he so faithfully depicted in his writing. Often it was a case of waiting patiently for a particular season or mood of the weather in order to capture photographically the matching quotation, but almost invariably I found that despite the accelerated advance of our twentieth century civilization the essential truth of Hardy's observation on scene or place remained much as he knew it. In one of his later poems, which in my opinion is one of his finest, *Afterwards*, Hardy posed the question:

When the Present has latched its postern behind my tremulous stay,
And the May month flaps its glad green leaves like wings,
Delicate-filmed as new-spun silk, will the neighbours say,
"He was a man who used to notice such things"?

I trust that from the photographs the readers will find ample evidence that not only was he *a man who used to notice such things,* but one who could express his joy in them and truthfully transmit the experience to others. As his friend Dr. Marie Stopes once noted: 'He reminded me of a red-breasted robin who, having caught a worm, looked brightly round sideways at one as though it would add to his pleasure if you ate it with him.'

In the text accompanying the photographs I have whenever possible allowed Hardy to speak for himself through direct quotations other than those linked with the photographs. To avoid the tedium and clutter of footnotes I have indicated solely with italics where Hardy's words are used. Almost without exception these statements are from the same work as the quotation illustrated, or else from his diaries, letters or notebook.

To supplement her map of the total area covered, my wife, Jenny, has drawn additional maps to help locate places off the main highways. Although most places are accessible to the general public, readers I am sure will appreciate that owners' permissions must be obtained to visit sites such as Tess's 'coffin' and the Greenwood Tree which are located on private land.

HARDY'S BIRTHPLACE

Few writers have furnished their fiction from the bric-a-brac of early family events as extensively as Thomas Hardy, and nowhere in all his novels and stories has this rich fund of family lore been used to more joyous effect than in his second published novel *Under the Greenwood Tree*. Though not so well constructed as the later novels, *The Mellstock Quire, A Rural Painting of the Dutch School,* as the book was sub-titled, floats lightly on the surface of life with the antic utterances and deeds of the church minstrels providing humorous accompaniment to Dick Dewy's courtship of village schoolmistress Fancy Day.

The Dewys' cottage described in the quotation is word for word the cottage in the photograph that Hardy's great-grandfather, John Hardy of Puddletown, built in the first year of the last century for the first of the three Thomas Hardys and his young bride. At the end of a lane that leads to nowhere, on the edge of the heath, it was both a home and place of business for his stone-mason grandparent and father, and here in the middle dormer-windowed bedroom the writer was born on June 2nd 1840.

In the course of those forty years that lone cottage to which the first Thomas Hardy had brought his young bride had become part of a small settled community known as New Bockhampton. There were now nine houses in the cherry tree-lined lane, and though grandfather Thomas had died three years earlier, three generations of Hardys now lived in the small cottage and a firm family tradition had been established. Thus from his grandmother and parents the writer had a wealth of colourful anecdotes concerning those years on which his imagination could feed, which together with his understanding and feeling for the countryside he was growing up in he could fashion into the fabric of his poems and novels. Here in this happy homestead he wrote his first five novels, from the unpublished *The Poor Man and the Lady* to his first acclaimed success *Far From the Madding Crowd*, much of the writing being done sitting in the window seat of the bedroom he shared with his brother, Henry (the right-hand dormer window in the picture).

Throughout his lifetime Hardy continued to visit and maintain an interest in his birthplace, even long after the last of the Hardys (his brother and sisters Mary and Kate) had left. As late as 1920, when his friend Hermann Lea was living there, he rearranged the garden which had been mainly grass and orchard into a floral knot of flower beds. But although imaginatively transforming events and experiences into his writing, he jealously guarded his private life against the intrusive prying of the public and press and sought to project his natural reticence beyond the grave. It was not his wish that his birthplace should become a museum and place of pilgrimage. He expressed the hope that its tenant should be a farm worker or artisan and his family; that the cottage should continue in its early tradition as a place where human joys and sorrows were contained, rather than as a static monument to his illustrious self.

Although Hardy's characteristically humble and sensible thoughts for the future of the cottage have not been fully realised – since 1947 the National Trust has been custodian of the small homestead at Higher Bockhampton, as it is now designated – his wishes have been met in one respect. It is still a lived-in home with a resident curator. Cottage and garden may be viewed from the vantage point that the photograph was taken from, and arrangements can be made to look over the low-ceilinged rooms, simply furnished in the period when it was Hardy's home, by appointment with the curator.

It was a long low cottage with a hipped roof of thatch having dormer windows breaking up into the eaves, a chimney standing in the middle of the ridge and another at each end.
UNDER THE GREENWOOD TREE

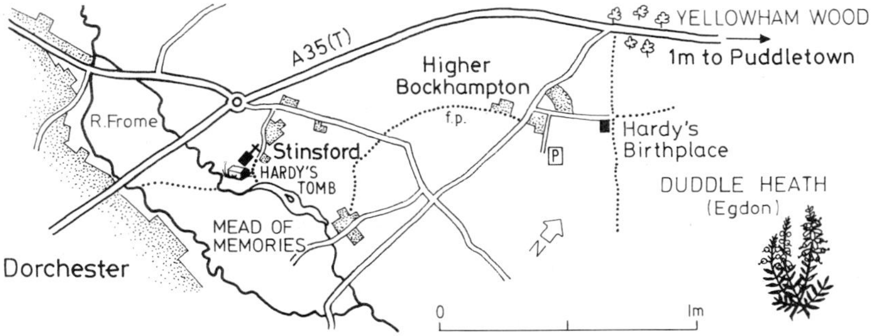

STINSFORD

The sad man's – the poet's – phantasy *The Dead Quire*, where Christmas Eve revellers in a dormered inn suddenly sobered by the old familiar carolling of the long since departed *Mellstock Quire* tumble out of the tavern in bemused pursuit of the recognised voices and viols,

Then did the Quick pursue the Dead
By crystal Froom that crinkles there;
And still the viewless quire ahead
Voiced the old holy air.

represents, somewhat paradoxically, Hardy in his happiest vein as a poet. For in these verses which he included in his *Time's Laughingstocks* collection, the writer, using as his setting what was for him the most familiar and best loved corner of his county, turned the tables on nostalgia to create a lively, amusing poem concluding on a mock ironic note.

As from a dream each sobered son
Awoke, and musing reached the door:
'Twas said that of them all, not one
Sat in a tavern more.

However, to return to the opening lines quoted with the photograph, the Mead of Memories just below the ascending Church-way in the foreground are the Frome-flanking meadows leading back to the small stone bridge at Lower Bockhampton; and to follow the footpath along from the bridge up to the church on a still summer's evening is to experience one of the most soothing and peaceful walks to be found anywhere in the English countryside. Were Hardy to return to this favourite walk of his, as he did many times after leaving the family home at Higher Bockhampton, he would find it as he continued to do throughout his long life – quite unchanged with scarcely a stick out of place.

Moaning Hill, a name possibly suggested to the poet by the wind soughing through the branches of a clump of chestnuts, indicates the short, steep road leading up from the church of St. Michael's, Stinsford, combining in its ancient stonework styles ranging from Transition-Norman to late Perpendicular. Though now stripped of its minstrel's gallery, there is preserved just inside the doorway a framed drawing made by Hardy under his father's supervision showing the arrangement, circa 1835, of the treble, tenor, counter and bass singers grouped around the four musicians, who then included grandfather Thomas Hardy (cello), father Thomas Hardy and Uncle James Hardy (violins).

The poet's own association with the church is commemorated by a beautiful stained glass window erected to his memory by public subscription, dramatically illustrating one of his favourite texts from the Book of Kings, 'And after the fire a still small voice . . . "What doest thou there, Elijah?"' The centre panel, depicting the purple-cloaked prophet, is flanked on the left by the wind-torn mountains with trees bowed over and snapping off, 'but the Lord was not in the wind' while the right panel with flashes of lightning and toppling castles vividly evokes the earthquake and fire that followed the wind. It is just right. A memorial preserving an intimate fragment of consciousness within the fabric of a revered building embodying the hopes and fears of many centuries that Hardy, could he have been consulted on the matter, would have certainly approved.

Beside the Mead of Memories,
Where Church-way mounts to Moaning Hill
The sad man sighed his phantasies:
He seems to sigh them still.

'THE GREENWOOD TREE'

Now somewhat hemmed in by younger growth, but nevertheless still very much as Hardy described it more than a century ago, the eponymous beech abutting on keeper Geoffrey Day's premises in *Yalbury Wood* suffered much indignity in subsequent years at the hands and knives of souvenir-hungry admirers of the writer. Since the 1939–45 War though, when Yell'ham Wood was host to American GIs, the venerable tree has been allowed to flourish in comparative obscurity as far as attacks on its limbs and leaves are concerned.

But the noble beech was severely slighted shortly after the war, when a photographer from a top national daily muffed an assignment and the paper published a photo of 'The Greenwood Tree' that plainly was not. Letters to the editor poured in, retraction and publication of another photograph, this time of the rightful claimant to the title, being the eventual outcome. As the real-life keeper occupying the cottage, Mr. E. S. L. Cutler, to whom I am indebted for the details of this incident, scornfully remarked, 'Tweren't even an English tree the chap photographed, but a blessed furriner – a Turkey oak.'

The photographer sent to repair the gaffe asked Mr. Cutler if he could be sure the tree pointed out was that intended by the writer. Recounting his reply he added with a chuckle, 'Sure? Why, many's the shilling I've had from Sir Thomas under the Greenwood Tree.' No doubt Hardy – 'A courteous, kindly old man. I often came across him poking around in the hedgerows with his stick. He was very interested in the different kinds of wild flowers.' – would have been equally amused and pleased by the honorary title conferred on him by a fellow Wessex countryman.

. . . an ancient tree, horizontally of enormous extent, though having no great pretensions to height.

UNDER THE GREENWOOD TREE

DORCHESTER, COUNTY MUSEUM

The grotesque stone mask that Mayor Henchard's daughter Elizabeth-Jane discovered in the back alley entrance to High Place Hall is a feature in the book that can no longer be seen in the setting in Dorchester where Hardy described it. This unusual keystone, which is probably of Roman origin, was saved when the archway was demolished after the last war, and since 1948 has been out of range of stone throwing schoolboys in a reconstructed arch in the county museum at Dorchester.

Hardy's concern for privacy even beyond the grave, already noted in respect to his Higher Bockhampton birth-place, extended equally to the mansion the successful writer built for himself and Emma at Max Gate. It was not to become a shrine through which a paying public might troop and disturb his ghost. It is fortunate therefore for those who would nevertheless like to get a little closer to the man behind the books that, largely through the behests of his second wife Florence, a room has been set aside in the museum where many of his personal effects are displayed.

The gape-mouthed mask high on the archway entrance looks down on display cases containing such memorabilia as his Order of Merit and various other medals presented to him, including the Silver Medal of the Intitute of British Architects, awarded in 1863. Amongst the small and intimate items that help to bring into focus this quiet, unassuming man, there is the plain, worn, silver pocket watch – the only watch he ever owned. There are period photographs, paintings (including some of his own early watercolours) and the original engravings that illustrated the novels when they first appeared as magazine serials, whilst across the width of the room at the far end is a reconstruction of his study at Max Gate.

The study in its total arrangement behind a glass screen transmits a powerful feeling of his presence, especially through the centrepiece – his desk. On the desk, almost as though he might have just left them there whilst he went for lunch, are his pince-nez, magnifying glasses, roll-blotter, pens and an ivory paper-knife, with a favourite walking stick leaning against the chair behind. The most poignant item on the desk, though, is his perpetual calendar set at March 7th, the day he and Emma first met. It remained at that date for the fifteen years he survived her, a constant reminder of his loss.

In a corner of the study are his violin and 'cello which, together with the neatly hand-notated music books in a case in the Hardy Room (hymns and carols entered from one end, secular tunes from the other until they meet in the middle), testify to the strong family musical tradition. Also, near his desk stands the small table on which his earlier works were written.

For every visitor to this well-arranged collection of Hardyana there will doubtless be one or more objects that will have particular significance. My own selection is something that was given to the writer in his later years – a finely constructed model of a full-rigged ship in a glass case. Hardy had once remarked to John Masefield that he had always wanted, but never possessed, a model ship. The former sailor who was at that time the country's Poet Laureate built this beautiful momento which he named 'The Triumph' from the second line of Hardy's poem *One We Knew – 'The Triumph', 'The New-rigged Ship',* and presented it to him. A small inscription on the hull of the vessel reads:

For Thomas Hardy Poet
from John Masefield poet
with admiration and homage.

This kindly gesture and humble recognition of his stature must I think have pleased Hardy as much as any of the honorary degrees and tributes that crowned his final years.

Originally the mask had exhibited a comic leer, as could still be discerned; but generations of Casterbridge boys had thrown stones at the mask, aiming at its open mouth; and the blows thereon had chipped off the lips and jaws as if they had been eaten away by disease.

THE MAYOR OF CASTERBRIDGE

DORCHESTER CEMETERY

Standing bare-headed in blinding, bitterly cold rain in Dorchester Cemetery on January 2nd 1924, Hardy, then 83 and having scorned the advice of friends to stay at home, watched a small urn being lowered into a glistening bed cut into the wet chalk. They were burying the ashes of his friend Sir Frederick Treves, a man he had known all his life (as a boy he had bought his first writing desk from Treves' father's shop) and no consideration for his own health could deter him from paying his last respects. Notched high on the yardstick of Hardy's character was the enduring quality of his fealty to friends, which carried over beyond the grave and to which he could give lasting metrical expression. Three days later his elegy, *In the Evening*, appeared in *The Times*. He survived the chill drenching to live another four productive years.

Sir Frederick Treves, Bart., GCVO, CB, Searjeant Surgeon to the King, whose book *Highways and Byways in Dorset* has been frequently quoted in these pages, shared more with Hardy than a life-long love of their native county. For also, in the measure of his wit and the acerbity of his digs at deserving, and occasionally undeserving, targets when he laid down lancet and picked up pen, he paralleled in his prose the shrewd directness of the poet-novelist. Their lives touched at many points and the Dorchester and near Dorchester-born writers naturally had several mutual literary friends, most notable from within their own county being William Barnes, the philologist and renowned Dorset dialect poet. As a boy Treves had attended the small school Barnes conducted in the county town, whilst in Barnes' later years spent at Came Rectory, a short distance from Hardy's house at Max Gate, the two poets kept in close touch, the younger established writer frequently consulting the elderly Wessex bard on matters relating to county lore and language.

But first and foremost Treves was a surgeon gifted with extraordinary skill. The drama of the appendicectomy he performed on Edward VII before his coronation–an operation delayed to danger point by the King's wish not to alarm or disappoint his people by cancelling his scheduled ceremonial drive through London – is an event that has since become fairly well known. Less known, far removed from the limelight of royal occasions, is an example of his manipulative prowess exercised at Lulworth Cove in his native Dorset. A small child had fallen from the top of the high sheer cliff there and, although her clothes catching as she fell had partly lessened the impact of the drop, nearly every bone in her young body was smashed. Treves, who had been picnicking nearby, worked with such sureness on her mangled frame that her recovery was complete and full use of all her limbs was restored. Hardy's acknowledgement of this god-like gift possessed by his friend is contained in the closing lines of his *Times* tribute, set into the base of the Celtic cross that marks his last resting place.

A marvellous Deftness called you forth – to do
Much that was due.
Good. You have returned. And all is well.

In the evening, when the world knew he was dead
He lay amid the dust and hoar
Of ages; and to a spirit attending said:
"This chalky bed? –
I surely seem to have been here before?"

FARINGDON

By way of contrast to Dorset's most prominent, well-known ruin at Corfe is the little-known and less written about Faringdon (or Farringdon) ruin at Winterborne Came near Dorchester. Not much to look at, certainly, just the east gable-end of what was once the fourteenth century church of St. Germains. But, representing all that remains of the former medieval village of Winterborne Faringdon, it has the attraction that vanished communities have for most of us who tend to think in terms of a continuous tradition of settlement. Hardy at any rate, who later built his house nearby at Max Gate (Mack's Gate), was intrigued enough by it to include it in his novel of the Napoleonic era *The Trumpet-Major*, and provided in the quoted fragment of dialogue an explanation of the village's extinction.

There were, of course, many medieval villages in Dorset that became deserted and gradually disappeared at different times for reasons not always known and seldom recorded. Periodic plagues were a not uncommon cause of a village's depopulation and decay, and such may have been the case with Faringdon, although there is a reference to the village in Hutchins' *History of Dorset* – a source frequently consulted by Hardy – that has a bearing on the avarice of the squirearchy as a possible reason for its obliteration.

Having noted that the church had become ruinous as early as 1648 when divine service ceased to be celebrated in it, Hutchins went on to quote from the *Survey of Dorsetshire*, attributed to John Coker but in fact compiled by Thomas Gerard of Trent, regarding the village. Anciently it had belonged to the Lords Galfrid, John, Robert and Thomas de Anno, Thomas giving the place together with the village of Tincleton and his daughter and co-heir Alice to a Robert de Farendon. In Gerard's time, Hutchins further quoted, it was 'a lone church, for there is hardlie anie house left in the parish, such of late hath beene the covetousnesse of some private men that, to increase their demesnes, have depopulated whole parishes.'

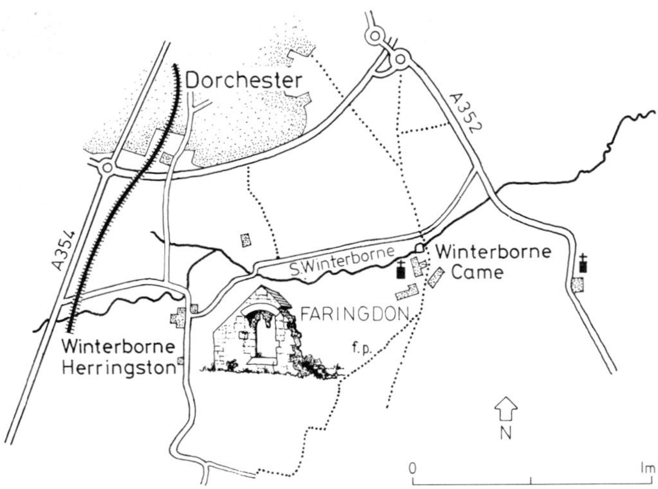

"Yes, this field used to be a village. My grandfather could call to mind when there were houses here. But the squire pulled 'em down, because poor folk were an eyesore to him."
THE TRUMPET-MAJOR

OSMINGTON WHITE HORSE

White Horses carved into chalk hillsides enliven the landscape at several points in the South of England, but pride of place is undoubtedly held by the prancing steed bearing George III up a hill overlooking Osmington, just outside Weymouth. Poor mad George, the patron sovereign of this Wessex spa – the monarch whose regular summer sojourns there put the place on the fashionable seaside resort map – endeared himself to the merchants of the town who consequently commissioned the carving, and the trumpet-major's homely explanation of the projected chalk monument's dimensions was no exaggeration since it measures 280 feet in length and is 323 feet high.

Yet why, if the figure was intended to express the gratitude of the loyal Weymouth citizens for the favour bestowed on their borough by his partiality to the invigorating qualities of the sea in their bay, is *King Jarge* depicted riding, not towards the town, but away in the direction of London?

To this question there are as many answers as there are White Horses, but the most popular explanation is that members of the Court, forced to share the Royal Family's annual summer at the seaside but having little enthusiasm for the provincial pleasures of *the King's watering-place,* conspired to have it carved that way as a gentle hint to George to get back to the more sophisticated life of his capital. A likely, likeable story with a wry, ironical twist that Hardy no doubt appreciated, it might even contain a grain of truth. Although 1798–1805 were the years during which Gloucester Lodge (now the Gloucester Hotel) was the royal summer residence and the effigy was not cut before 1807–8, the King continued to make Hardy's *Budmouth* his summer home up until the eve of Waterloo.

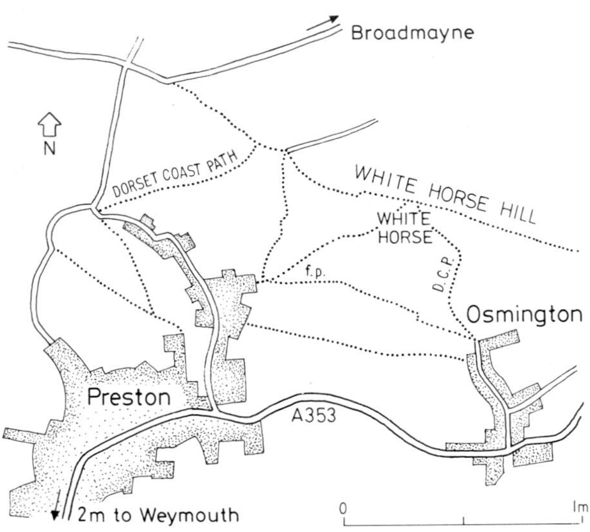

"The king's head is to be as big as our mill-pond and his body as big as this garden; he and the horse will cover more than an acre."

THE TRUMPET-MAJOR

PORTLAND

Portland – *the peninsula carved by Time out of a single stone,* and for centuries carved out by men who have valued that stone for its beauty, strength and durability as a building material (Wren, whilst building St. Paul's was concerned that supplies might be exhausted before his Cathedral was completed) is undoubtedly one of the most fascinating natural features of the Wessex scene. *Connected with the mainland by a long thin neck of pebbles 'cast up by the rages of the se,'* it is both geologically unique and historically redoubtable. The islanders, forced to accept the Norman takeover but retaining to the present day their separate, unassimilable identity, rebuffed raids by the Danes in the eighth century and incursions by the French in the eighteenth and nineteenth. Significantly, it was from Portland that the bulk of the American forces sailed for the liberation of Occupied Europe.

Viewed across a calm, sun-lit sea from the vicinity of Lulworth Cove, the rocky fastness displays a serenity that belies the elemental strife that has shaped the character of its people. Whilst its eastern flank provides a safe anchorage for the Portland naval base, the western shore takes the brunt of the not infrequent wild weather that sweeps up Channel from the south-west. Then too, off the Bill or Beale Point, the swift and treacherous Portland Race has caught many a craft unawares to add it to the countless toll of wrecks that have foundered there or been driven up onto its chesil coastline.

Yet, almost treeless, with only a scratching of soil to cover its barren rock, it is nevertheless a remarkably interesting place to visit. Fortuneswell, its principal town, clambering up the steep slope of its northern approach, with *houses above houses, one man's doorstep rising behind his neighbour's chimney, the gardens hung up by one edge to the sky,* bears mute testimony to the tenacity of the islanders. And throughout the peninsula the houses, shops, inns and cottages, built alike of the weathered native stone, display with their gaily coloured doors, window shutters and windowbox gardens a determination to triumph over the general bleakness of the environment.

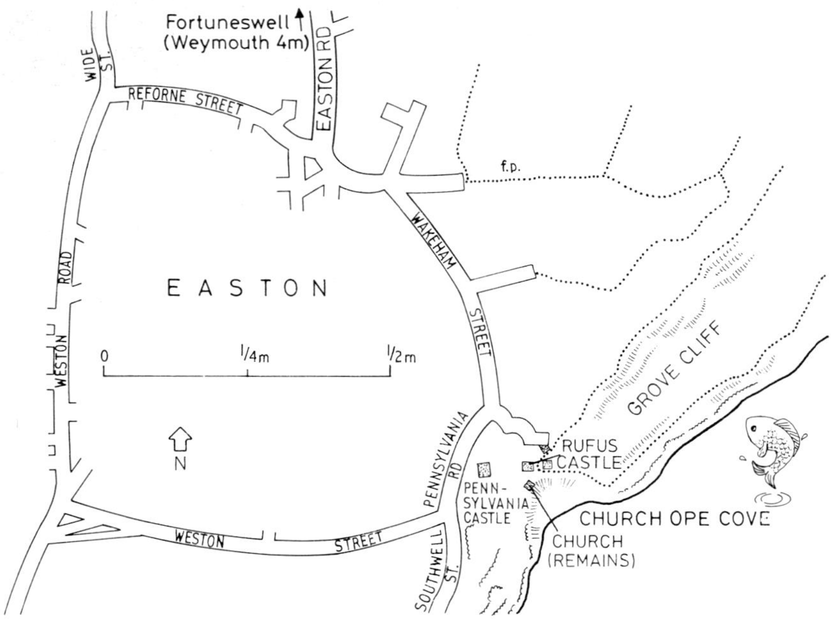

That Gibraltar of Wessex, the singular peninsula once an island, and still called such, that stretches out like the head of a bird into the English Channel.

THE WELL-BELOVED

PENNSYLVANIA CASTLE

Pennsylvania Castle, Portland, Dorset – a transatlantic transplant in reverse? Some eccentric English millionaire's folly? The re-erection of an American frontier fort on the craggy Dorset coast perhaps? Such guesses generated by the name of this building are likely to seem less than wild when the castle is first encountered, for it is obviously of no great antiquity. However Hardy, who chose it as a summer residence for his constant courtier hero Jocelyn Pierston, by trimming its title to the original Sylvania stressed the quite English derivation of its name. Sylvania acknowledges the sheltering trees – the only trees on this rocky promontory – that afford the castle some protection from the blustery winds that rake the Portland peninsula, trees that were planted either by John Penn, a former Governor of the Isle of Portland for whom the castle was built at the beginning of the nineteenth century, or by his friend George III.

Yet even though it has acquired its name independently, there is a family link between the castle and its namesake state as John Penn was the grandson of William Penn, the state's founder.

With impressive coastal views from most of its rooms, the castle is now a comfortable hotel, providing a good base from which to explore this rugged Wessex appendage.

Sylvania Castle, a dignified manor-house in a nook by the cliffs with modern castellations and battlements.
THE WELL-BELOVED

RUFUS CASTLE

Considering its size – four miles long and no more than a mile and a half across at its widest point – Portland is well provided with castles, but of its several fortresses the gaunt keep of Rufus Castle, perched high on the edge of a cliff on its eastern flank, is the oldest and most enigmatic. Was there ever more than just the castle keep? Have other parts crumbled down the cliff to the sea below? The early records are few and throw little light onto the mystery of its origin.

It is known that in 1142 Robert, Earl of Gloucester, took possession of it from King Stephen for the Empress Matilda (or Maud), and therefore probable that William Rufus, the Red King, erected it perhaps half a century previously. But what purpose did it serve? Bearing in mind the fierce independence of the inhabitants of the *Isle of Slingers* and that William of Normandy's conquest did not include all corners of the realm, it is possible that Portland was only brought under Norman control during Rufus' reign and that he built the castle to garrison the peninsula. A local tradition maintains that it was erected as a place of refuge for the inhabitants, although never completed. This again might well be true, since from Saxon times the islanders were frequently harried by Danish raiders.

Whatever the reason for its erection, to protect or subject the islanders, the solid old remnant, romantic by moonlight and daytime challenge to exploration-minded boys, symbolises in its defiant cliff-edge stance those tough enduring qualities characteristic of this *rocky coign of England.*

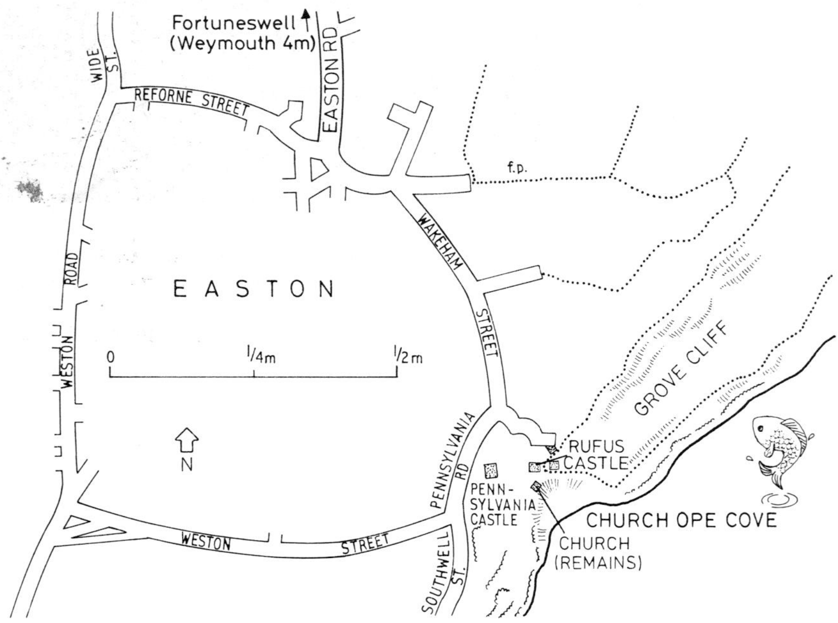

. . . the ruin of the Red King's or Bow-and-Arrow Castle, standing as a square black mass against the moonlit, indefinite sea.

THE WELL-BELOVED

CHURCH OPE

Ope Churchyard, to lop off the aspirate and restore the rightful name to this disappearing Portland feature, provided Hardy with an ideal symbol to employ in the strangest of his novels of Wessex life. His use of it, however, did not exactly endear him to a large sector of his late-Victorian reading public, particularly when he elaborated on one of the Island *mores* and made reference to the old Portland custom of delaying marriage until the intended wife was pregnant. Yet, as with all his writing, his intention had been merely to pass on information that he considered interesting and relevant.

To 'kimberlins', those not native to the *Isle of Slingers,* the custom might admittedly appear not quite by the book, but to the extremely independent islanders, a small close community concerned with maintaining their separate identity, such cautious approach to the marriage union made very good sense. They had a code that was essentially as strict as that of the mainland, the main difference being that disgrace in their eyes was incurred if a wife falsely assured her man that she had conceived and a childless marriage ensued.

As partly can be seen, the churchyard together with the ruins of the church was when I photographed it well on the way to full oblivion, brambles and other wild growth completing the obliterating process initiated by the landslip – the symbol disappearing like most of the customs referred to by Hardy. But fortunately in recent years steps have been taken to preserve the church ruins and tumbled tombstones much as the landslip left them.

Below this point lies the secluded beach of Church Ope Cove (ope – an early Saxon word for opening), whilst standing out on the skyline at the top of the picture is the castle remnant known as Rufus or Bow-and-Arrow Castle, featured on the previous page.

Hope Churchyard, which lay in a ravine formed by a landslip ages ago . . . It seemed to say that in this last local stronghold of the Pagan divinities, where Pagan customs lingered yet, Christianity had established itself precariously at best.

THE WELL-BELOVED

PORTESHAM

From his home at Max Gate near Dorchester, Thomas Hardy the writer could see clearly the ugly, meaningless monument to Thomas Hardy the sailor – Nelson's Hardy – which towers like a land-locked lighthouse above Black Down Hill. Justly proud of his illustrious nautical namesake – he had an engraving of Sir Thomas Masterman Hardy in his drawing room – it was natural that he should wish somehow to work him into the framework of one of his novels, arranging in *The Trumpet-Major* to have Bob Loveday hike across to the Captain's house at Portesham to request a berth on the *Victory* prior to the momentous battle.

While engaged on the novel, and later during the creation of his epic peom *The Dynasts,* the author corresponded with Admiral Hardy's daughter on matters relating to her father's life and ancestry. Their respective families he felt were undoubtedly descended from one of the Jersey le Hardys who had settled in Dorset sometime in the fifteenth century. *The branches are always asserted locally to be connected, and no doubt are,* he wrote once to someone who had questioned him on the matter, adding that *my great-uncle knew the ramifications.*

Nestling below Black Down, snug in a cleft between hills surmounted by prehistoric stone curiosities, is the unspoilt village of Portesham – rough stone and thatch, large shady trees and quiet winding roads – providing in its charm and simplicity a more fitting memorial to the gallant seaman than the blatant official monument. In the house in the lower photograph he spent much of his boyhood before going to sea at the age of twelve, and he often returned to stay there between voyages, retaining to the end of his days a fond regard for 'Possum' – his version of the local dialect rendering of the village's name.

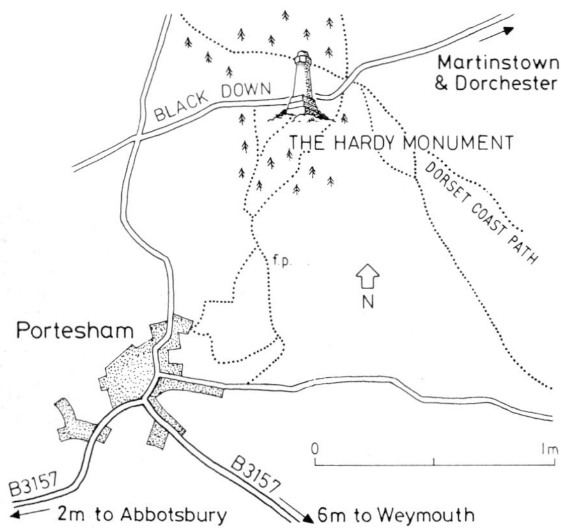

Pos'ham – the village of Captain Hardy's infancy.
THE TRUMPET-MAJOR

THE CERNE ABBAS GIANT

Goaded to desperate courage they waylaid and killed him, afterwards cutting his effigy on the hill, Hardy continued, jotting down in his notebook just one of the country legends associated with the enviable old Cerne Abbas giant. With his hundred and twenty foot hickory club held above his shrunken head (proportioning of parts was obviously not a particular skill that his carvers excelled in), the hundred and eighty foot chalk-outlined effigy has been the cause of much ribald comment, not to mention incredulous polishing of spectacles by maiden aunts taking a Sunday outing through the beautiful Cerne Valley.

The odd thing is, having written a note on the Giant, Hardy made no serious attempt to include a reference to him in one of his stories or novels. With the legends and superstitions that pertain to him it is strange that the monstrous figure was not somehow made use of by a writer who introduced such local oddities into his fiction wherever possible. But perhaps, even though a fearless foe of canting criticism, Hardy, aware of the shocked Victorian attitude to this notable landscape leviathan – prints of the period always portrayed him innocuously sexless – felt that since he probably would not be allowed to give a true picture of the Giant he would simply leave him on his hillside where centuries of rabbits have nibbled and burrowed beneath his anatomy.

It is not known with any certainty just when or by whom he was carved, but he was already there when the Romans arrived on the scene. They, naturally enough, associated him with the worship of Hercules, although the most likely explanation of his presence is a fertility symbol. The farmland valley he presides over coupled with the emphasis given to his virility would seem to indicate such intention on the part of his originators, and the subsequent site for an abbey at Cerne could possibly have been expressly chosen by the early English Christians to counteract the pagan beliefs.

Henry VIII dissolved the Abbey. Little beside the old gatehouse remains, although the village itself is one of the most picturesque in Dorset. The rude old Giant, cared for since 1920 by the National Trust, is likely to be there for a long time yet.

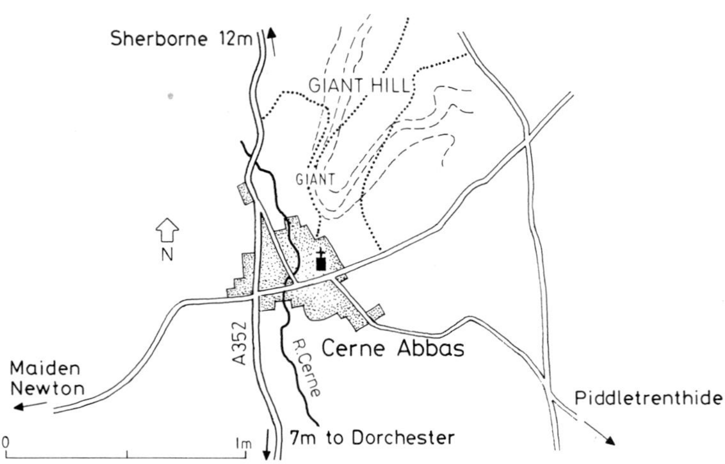

He threatened to descend upon Cerne and to ravish all the young maidens on a particular night and to kill the young men the next day.

THE FIRST NOTEBOOK

BATCOMBE CROSS AND HAND

Standing alone by a little-used road on a desolate upland near Batcombe – *so far removed from the charm which is sought in landscape as to reach a new kind of beauty, a negative beauty of tragic tone* – the moss-mottled, time-weathered pillar Cross and Hand, or Christ in Hand, has understandably drawn to itself a wealth of local legend and fanciful conjecture.

Through the solitary shepherd's explanation of its origin in reply to Tess's enquiry whether it ever was a Holy Cross, Hardy gave an example of the lone stone's power to evoke a more pagan response to the enigma of its purpose. But in his poem *The Lost Pyx,* the writer relates a less violent tradition. On a wild and stormy night, a priest from nearby Cerne Abbey was called out to shrive a dying man in his remote upland cottage. After stumbling through the storm, the priest discovered on arrival that he had dropped the sacrament somewhere en route, and with little hope of finding it retraced his steps. But there where he later raised the stone to commemorate the wonder of Christ in Hand, he found the pyx protected by a circling throng of wild beasts, *kneeling at gaze, in pause profound,* and sheltering it from the elements.

However, whatever its origins – holy or pagan (some antiquaries have noted that it has features in common with other pillars found among the remains of Roman temples in the area), the most likely explanation of its present siting would appear to be the purely utilitarian one of marking a boundary; a government bench-mark chiselled into its south face displaying officialdom's unconcern with its former associations.

"'Tis a thing of ill-omen, Miss. It was put up in wuld times by the relations of a malefactor who was tortured there by nailing his hands to a post and afterwards hung. The bones lie underneath. They say he sold his soul to the devil, and that he walks at times."

TESS OF THE D'URBERVILLES

'EGDON HEATH'

Hardy's bleak *Egdon Heath* – the wasteland comprising several tracts of open moors in the southern part of Dorset, divided by small planted forests and areas brought under cultivation, yet *virtually one in character and aspect* – is a territory often featured in his stories, novels and poetry. Undoubtedly he found in the desolation of its emptiness the natural counterpart of the human slough of despond, and certainly in *The Return of the Native* where the whole drama of passion and conflict is enacted against its sombre setting he eloquently elaborated the anthropomorphitic attributes of the heath so that it attains to a shadowy presence, the dark god moving behind the consciousness of the human actors. *The storm was its lover, and the wind its friend,* he wrote, and again, stressing its caliginous quality: *The face of the Heath by its mere complexion added half an hour to evening; it could in like manner retard the dawn, sadden noon, anticipate the frowning of storms scarcely generated, and intensify the opacity of a moon-midnight to a cause of shaking and dread.*

Right at the beginning of the novel – *It had a lonely face, suggesting tragical possibilities* – Hardy prepared his readers for the culminating climax in which the proud and passionate Eustacia Vye and her lover Damon Wildeve drown in a dark pool on the heath. The writer's observation on the tragic propensity of the frowning heath, though, had a particular relevance outside the realm of fiction in the life, or rather violent death, of his friend and staunch admirer T. E. Lawrence. It was as he scorched across this heath on his 'ton-up' Brough 'Boanerges' (Son of thunder – Mark III, v.7) that Lawrence, who had been a frequent visitor to Max Gate, having survived the perilous exploits of his Arabian Desert campaign and recently completed his service as an R.A.F. aircraftsman, swerved to avoid an errand boy and crashed to his death. His grave is in the little cemetery at Moreton on the edge of the heath. The cottage retreat he was speeding back to, Clouds Hill, not far from Bovington Camp, is cared for by the National Trust.

Though nowadays nuclear reactors hum in Egdon's heart, the grappling tracks of tanks churn part of its flint and heather surface to a furrowed bareness and shells whine over a restricted area of its southern flank, the heath retains its general bleakness of aspect – *a place perfectly accordant with man's nature – neither ghastly, hateful, nor ugly; neither commonplace, unmeaning, nor tame; but, like man, slighted and enduring; and withal singularly colossal and mysterious in its swarthy monotony.*

A FACE ON WHICH TIME MAKES BUT LITTLE IMPRESSION . . . As with some persons who have long lived apart, solitude seemed to look out of its countenance. It had a lonely face, suggesting tragical possibilities.

THE RETURN OF THE NATIVE

BLACKMOOR VALE

A*n engirdled and secluded region . . . it is a vale whose acquaintance is best made by viewing it from the summits of the hills that surround it,* Hardy advised, introducing the reader to the beautiful Vale of Blakemore or Blackmoor, Tess's home valley *in which the fields are never brown and the springs never dry*. Unlike the *Valley of the Great Dairies* – the Frome Valley, Blackmoor – the *Vale of the Little Dairies* is not a wide alluvial plain fashioned by the sweep of a once broad river, but an uneven, irregular indentation arcing across the north-western corner of Dorset. No single river dominates its declivity, but innumerable nameless streams and a few slightly larger water courses – Caundle Brook, the Cam, Wriggle River – trickle through its dales within dales to water the sloping meadows which stretch away from the steep chalk ridge forming its southern flank.

The alternative, somewhat contrasting name for the valley – White Hart Vale – dates from a period when that part of the country was densely wooded, and derives from a legend concerning 'a beautiful and goodly white hart' that Henry III encountered while hunting in the region. Having spared the animal's life, he was furious when he later learned that the Bailiff of Blackmoor, Sir Thomas de la Lynde, a huntsman quite lacking in the manner of aesthetics, had slain the rare and graceful creature. Not only were de la Lynde and his men thrown into gaol and heavily fined, but thereafter the king levied an annual tax known as the 'white hart silver' on the squires and yeomen of the vale to atone for the thoughtless deed.

The typical view of tidy fields and copse-crowned hillocks is from Dungeon Hill, a short distance from King's Stag, where, at the site of a small stone bridge crossing the River Lydden – a bridge that still has a sign borne by many old Dorset bridges, sternly threatening transportation for anyone found damaging its stones – the white hart is believed to have been killed.

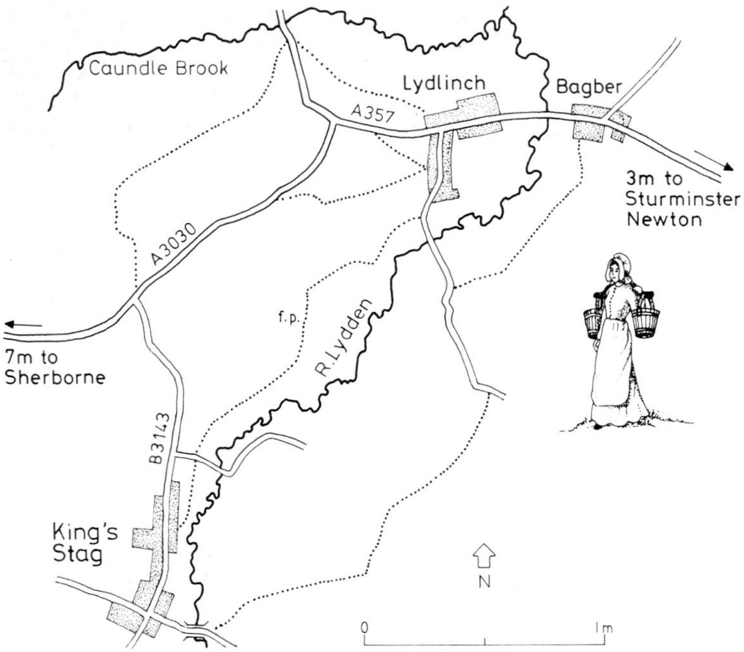

Here, in the valley, the world seems to be constructed upon a smaller and more delicate scale . . . the prospect is a broad rich mass of grass and trees, mantling minor hills and dales within the major. Such is the Vale of Blackmoor.

TESS OF THE D'URBERVILLES

BERE REGIS PARISH CHURCH

Under the church of that there parish lie my ancestors – hundreds of 'em – in coats of mail and jewels, in gr't lead coffins weighing tons and tons. There's not a man in the county o' South-Wessex that's got grander and nobler skillentons in his family than I.

The irrepressible John Durbeyfield's proud boast after learning from Pa'son Tringham of his lapsed lineage – the unfortunate information that triggered off his daughter Tess's tragedy, and which later provided his happy child-like wife Joan and her homeless young family with the incongruous temporary solution of camping out in their old four-poster bed near the family vault – is just one of the many lighter features of the author's most widely read novel. But the historical base on which Hardy built his fictional romance can, here in the Parish Church of Bere Regis, readily be identified. Visitors to this extremely interesting church, with its twelve carved Apostles horizontally poised and peering down from the ornate 15th century nave roof trusses, may read on a brass plate in the south aisle:

'Here lies Robert Turberville, arm bearer, who in his lifetime united that part of the Manor of Bere Regis which belonged to Tarrant Abbey before its dissolution, to the part which he had inherited from his forefathers who had been lords of the manor from ancient times. This said Robert died April 5th A.D. 1559. Be merciful Christ Jesus.'

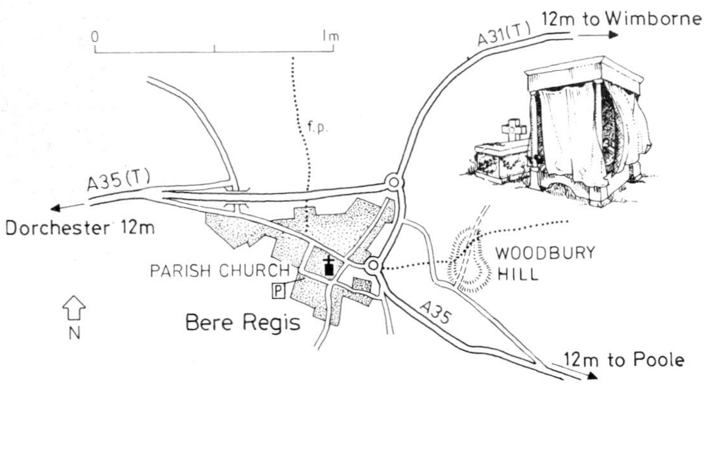

Hard by, the aisle of the church called the d'Urberville Aisle looked on imperturbably.

TESS OF THE D'URBERVILLES

BERE REGIS

Also referred to by Hardy as *the half-dead townlet*, and by his friend Sir Frederick Treves in his *Highways and Byways in Dorset* as 'a dull village adrift in a duller country . . . a village of sackcloth which has taken upon itself a vow of silence,' Bere Regis one feels has been treated less than kindly by her county chroniclers. Although admittedly not today one of the most picturesque Wessex villages, the reference to sackcloth is oddly apposite, the place having been reduced largely to ashes by a fire in 1788. Hence the dearth of quaint and historical buildings – the vow of silence.

In the past though, Kyngsbere, or King's Bere as it was variously known, knew days that were neither silent nor dull, its purlieus often echoing to the horn of that hunting-mad monarch King John, who made it his base while pursuing the deer in the surrounding countryside. A local tradition claims John even had a castle there, although the records refer only to a manor house for the use of King and Court when hunting in the vicinity. Queen Elfrida was another royal with a residence at Bere, to which place she speedily retired to attempt to establish an alibi after the treacherous murder of her stepson Edward the Martyr at Corfe Castle in 978.

Appearing in the picture at the end of the High Street less dominating than in actuality is Woodbury Hill, an ancient British earthwork believed to date from the Iron Age, greenly providing further testimony to the former importance of the place. For centuries the setting of the annual Sheep Fair so colourfully described by Hardy in *Far From the Madding Crowd*, some measure of the old tradition still survives in a yearly fun fair held in the fields of its lower slopes.

Kingsbere-sub-Greenhill –
'a little one-eyed, blinking sort o'place.'
TESS OF THE D'URBERVILLES

MORETON

By using a phonetic spelling for the river Frome Hardy was lending a helping tongue to the non-Wessex reader and traveller, who might understandably expect Dorset's second river to rhyme with Rome. This swift-flowing river, watering the *Valley of the Great Dairies – in which milk and butter grew to rankness,* was very close to the author's heart. He was born just a mile from its banks, used to wander across the meadows to the Stinsford Church where his grandfather, father and uncle had played for the choir in the minstrel's gallery, and often featured it in his writing.

In Hardy's best-known novel the river is constantly encountered threading through the narrative. From Tess's first meeting with Angel Clare while working as a dairymaid in the *Froom* meads at *Talbothays* farm, to their disastrous *Wellbridge* honeymoon with Angel's perilous somnambulistic crossing of the plank bridge and Tess's wish that they might fall and be drowned in its deep, dark waters, the swift, serpentining stream provides a natural accompaniment to their courtship and the dividing climax of its unconsummated conclusion.

Illustrating the quotation from the novel, the picture is taken a couple of miles downstream from the imagined location of the *Talbothays* farm, near the village of Moreton where the widening river is shallow enough to be forded and rushes grow in abundance along its banks. Hardy's friend T. E. Lawrence is buried nearby in Moreton's small cemetery.

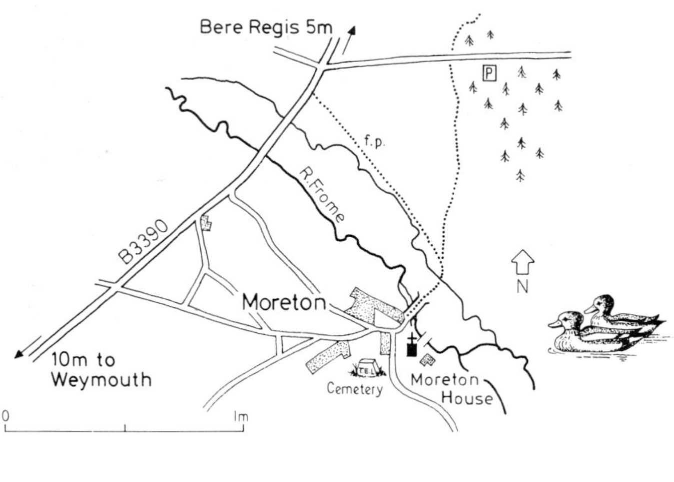

The Froom waters – clear as the pure River of Life shown to the Evangelist, rapid as the shadow of a cloud, with pebbly shallows that prattled to the sky all day long.

TESS OF THE D'URBERVILLES

STURMINSTER NEWTON

In contrast to the fast-flowing Frome, the Stour, Dorset's principal river, meanders in a more leisurely, dignified manner in its diagonal west/east crossing of the county. Early in its course where the river loops round the small market town of Sturminster Newton, near the birthplace of William Barnes, Hardy and his wife Emma established their first home. In the two years spent there at 'Riverside Villa' overlooking the Stour, years that he later looked back on as *our happiest time*, Hardy wrote some of his finest poems, his novel *The Return of the Native* being also written during that period.

His onomatopoeic poem *On Sturminster Foot-bridge* confused some of his critics, one of whom jested that the syllables of the verse sounded like milk slopping in a cart. Had this reviewer paused to consider the significance of his comment he would have realised that his jest was a true word spoken, a recognition of Hardy's achievement, for the sound he had scornfully selected was just such as the poet was aiming for – the clucking of ripples when the river was blown upon by an upstream wind.

Erected by J. Conway in 1841, the foot-bridge remains substantially as when it was built, a narrow span providing a link for the leisurely with footpaths across open meadows and common land.

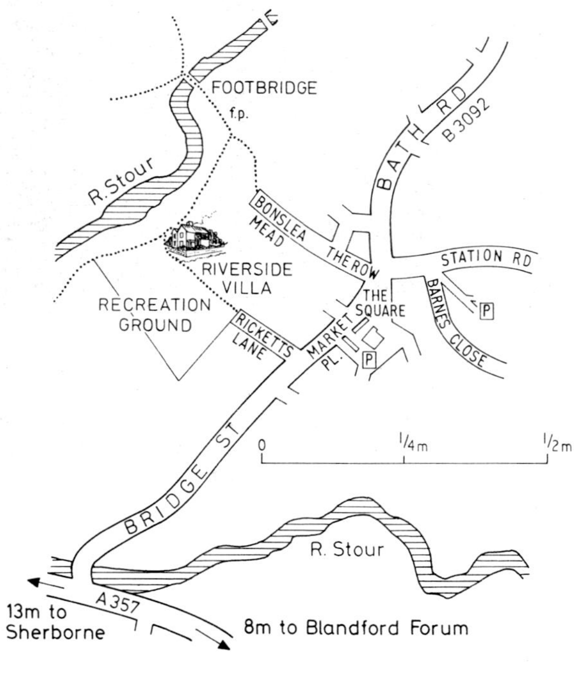

Reticulations creep upon the slack stream's face
When the wind skims irritably past,
The current clucks smartly into each hollow place
That years of flood have scrabbled in the pier's sodden base;
The floating-lily leaves rot fast.

SHAFTESBURY

Still sometimes referred to as Shaston by its older inhabitants and economically spelt that way on the milestones, King Alfred's hill-top Shaftesbury may well be *now world-forgotten and virtually unvisited,* although not forgetful in its dream of centuries of its youthful prime – jagged evidence of which still juts out in places. The surviving portion of old town wall, providing a sun-trapping screen for the unhistorical cat drowsing in the somnolence of a Sunday afternoon on the warm, smooth cobbles of steep Gold Hill, dates back to Saxon times.

At the time of writing *Jude* – having selected *this breezy and whimsical spot* as the locale for Sue Bridehead's unfortunate marriage with Jude's boyhood exemplar Phillotson – Hardy bemoaned the destruction of the magnificient Abbey, which had through the Middle Ages brought the city such glory and renown. At the Dissolution the enormous Abbey, which had contained the carefully preserved relics of King Edward the Martyr, was destroyed. *The Martyr's bones,* Hardy sadly noted, *met with the fate of the sacred pile that held them, not a stone being left to tell where they lie.* However, in 1931, just three years after the writer's death, a small leaden casket was unearthed on the site and found to contain the bones of this treacherously murdered king, removed from its shrine and hidden by the nuns at the time of Henry the Eighth's edict; a tidy historical footnote that would have pleased the novelist-poet, much of whose inspiration stemmed from a keen awareness of the rich and colourful past of the region in which he was born.

SHASTON, the ancient British Palladour . . . in itself the city of a dream.

JUDE THE OBSCURE

SALISBURY

To the present day traveller, caught up in the confusion of traffic choking the narrow streets and unable to appreciate fully the timbered charm of Salisbury's many fine Tudor buildings owing to the bewilderment of signs directing him to other places, denying him entry, prohibiting his halting and otherwise distracting and distressing him, the adjectives quiet and soothing may not at first appear apposite, even remotely applicable. But pass through either of the three medieval gateways into the spacious, wide-lawned Cathedral Close with its sheltering tall elm trees and the truth of Hardy's statement, written towards the end of the more leisurely last century, is immediately appreciated mid the hurly-burly of the present one.

Viewed from whatever angle (in this instance from the vicinity of the fifteenth century King's House, formerly used by royalty when travelling through the south-west – the Training College that Hardy's sisters attended and from which Sue Bridehead was expelled), Bishop Richard Poore's graceful thirteenth century cathedral with its mellowed limestone façade and finely-tapering 404 foot spire – *the most marked instance in England of an architectural intention carried out to the full* – never fails to evoke the mood of contemplative calm that for centuries characterised the city set among meadows in a crook of the Wiltshire Avon. The city originally known as New Saresbury is that for which Hardy coined the name Melchester.

"The Cathedral has had its day! . . . The Cathedral was a very good place four or five centuries ago; but it is played out now . . .' Sue's denunciatory outburst venting her resentment of the fusty medieval environment in which much of her young life had been spent was seized on by some critics and commentators at the time as a direct expression of Hardy's own views regarding the Cathedral. A rather odd assumption, for although admittedly a great deal of Hardy's reflection on matters ecclesiastical was embodied in Sue's character, his feelings towards the Cathedral came closer to Jude's non-intellectual attachment to the charm of its delicately carved stonework and the beauty of its setting. Salisbury was a city that he never tired of visiting, and an entry in his diary recording a visit to the Cathedral late at night perfectly captures the poetry of such occasions.

The moon was visible through both the north and south clerestory windows to me standing on the turf on the north side. . . . Walked to the west front, and watched the moonlight creep round upon the statuary of the façade – stroking tentatively and then more and more firmly the prophets, the martyrs, the bishops, the kings, and the queens . . . Upon the whole the Close of Salisbury, under a full summer moon on a windless midnight, is as beautiful a scene as any I know in England – or for the matter of that elsewhere.

Melchester was a quiet and soothing place.
JUDE THE OBSCURE

STONEHENGE

By choosing Wessex's most remarkable temple as the scene for his heroine's dawn arrest Hardy was being more than merely dramatic, for the parallel between the innocent Tess's fate and that of a selected victim slaughtered to the sun god is hard to overlook. For her final hours of freedom with the man she loved and who had failed her, the author set Tess against the prehistoric background of ritualistic sacrifice; a hapless victim of a society that, although outwardly civilised, shared with the earlier tribes a fair measure of the calculating cruelty that appears to belong to mankind throughout all its ages and stages.

I often think of the day when, having decided that she must die, Hardy later stated, *I went purposely to Stonehenge to study the spot. It was a gloomy lowering day, and the skies almost seemed to touch the pillars of the great heathen temple.* And such is often the case with this ancient edifice standing out on the empty expanse of Salisbury Plain. Oddly enough, to see the stone circles in bright sunlight robs this temple to the sun of a certain amount of the awe it is capable of generating at other times.

In the picture the mid-summer sun can be seen to have just risen above the Heelstone or Sunstone framed in the centre trilithon which forms the entrance to the temple, whilst unseen but lying midway between the entrance and the Heelstone is the Slaughter Stone. At such times, at the extremes of dawn and dusk, the towering pillars make their deepest impression on the mind of the viewer. As Hardy himself remarked after a subsequent visit to Stonehenge, *The misfortune of ruins – to be beheld nearly always at noonday by visitors, and not at twilight.*

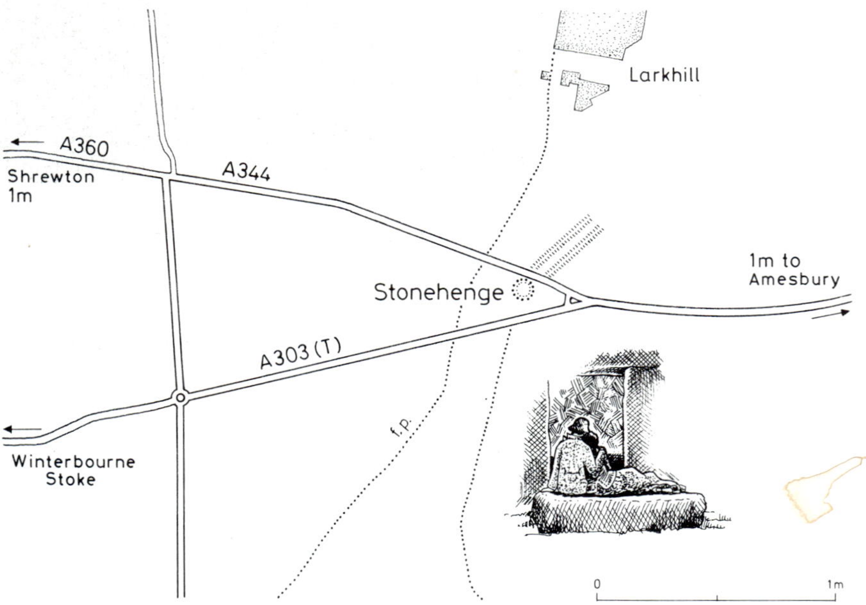

'Did they sacrifice to God here?' asked she.
'No,' said he.
'Who to?'
'I believe to the sun.'

TESS OF THE D'URBERVILLES

BOURNEMOUTH

The crusty residents of the town selected for Tess's ultimate tragedy – Hardy's Sandbourne, Hampshire's Bournemouth – doubtless took grave exception to the author's choice of their fair, exclusive spa as the setting for the fatal stabbing of her tormentor and betrayer Alec d'Urberville. So closely were the serialised novels followed, so near to real-life persons were the characters identified in the minds of the readers, that the foul deed could not have failed to bring the wrong sort of publicity to the resort – a tarnishing blemish on the *Pulchritudo et Salubritas* escutcheon. In recent times of course, the town has not altogether escaped the glare of the sensationalist press spot-light and murders more vile and less motivated than Tess's cathartic crime are known to have occurred there. But then that is going beyond the bounds of fiction, and times certainly change even if human passions and perversions remain more or less constant.

Today the *fairy place* quality of the seaside town that is now within the Dorset boundary can still be realised in many scenes such as that shown – Boscombe Chine Gardens on an August afternoon, although the writer's subtle gibe of *allowed to get a little dusty* won't do for the present day. With towering modern hotels and flats raking the cliff-top skyline, motor rally trials along the promenade, Davis Cup tournaments, conferences, conventions and the sheer volume of bucket and spade brigades descending upon the beaches, little dust, literally or figuratively, has much chance of settling. Though to the author of this book, who was born in the town and grew up there between the wars, recollections of its lingering Edwardian atmosphere exemplified by the hand-drawn hackney Bath-chairs being trundled through the avenues are much in accordance with Hardy's earlier observation. Certainly, in more than just country ways, *"He was a man that used to notice such things."*

This fashionable watering-place, with its eastern and its western stations, its piers, its groves of pines, its promenades, and its covered gardens . . . like a fairy place suddenly created by the stroke of a wand, and allowed to get a little dusty.

TESS OF THE D'URBERVILLES

TREBARWITH STRAND

The Atlantic-whipped, steep-cliffed stretch of coastline in North Cornwall used as the setting for his third novel, *A Pair of Blue Eyes,* the West that Emma Lavinia Gifford his *very West-of-Wessex girl* opened to him, contrasted strongly with the more tranquil scenery of Hardy's native Dorset, and in poetry powerfully evoking its elemental strife he gave full expression to the wild splendour of the Lower Wessex region. *The place is pre-eminently (for one person at least) the region of dream and mystery,* he wrote in the Preface to *A Pair of Blue Eyes. She Opened the Door,* a poem written in the year following Emma's death, acknowledged the debt to his departed wife for familiarising him with such a countryside. But more than that. Had she not encouraged him to persevere with his writing, he might well have abandoned his early, discouraging and frustrating advances in that direction to settle for the safer architectural career that had first brought him within her orbit.

She opened the door of Romance to me,
The door from a cell
I had known too well,
Too long, till then, and was fain to flee.

In the picture, withstanding the assault of the incoming tide, Trebarwith Strand (the *Barwith Strand* of *A Pair of Blue Eyes*) with the bird-owned islet Gull Rock hove-to on the horizon.

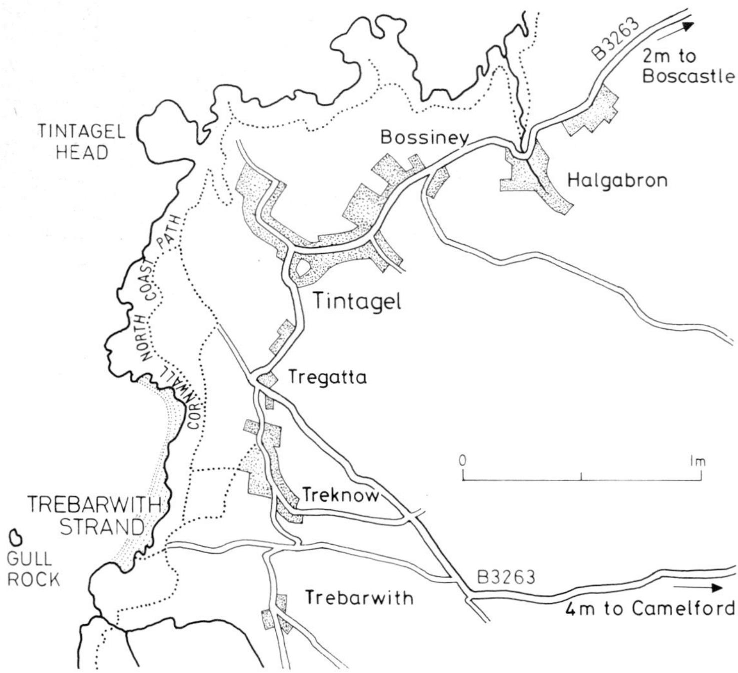

She opened the door of the west to me,
With its loud sea-lashings,
And cliff-side clashings
Of waters rife with revelry.

VALENCY VALLEY

In his poem *Under the Waterfall,* written years after the event, Hardy was recalling an incident from the time when he was courting his future wife Emma at the St. Juliot rectory. Picnicking in the secluded Valency Valley, they had dropped and been unable to retrieve a small drinking tumbler below a miniature waterfall; and around the romance of a lovers' shared chalice caught in a crevice of rock and worn smooth over the years by the cascading waters – *the rhyme of love persistently sung by the fall above* – he constructed a framework of verse immortalising the event, including it among the *Lyrics and Reveries* of his *Satires of Circumstance.* (He also, at the time of the picnic, made a pencil sketch of Emma inelegantly attempting to locate the lost glass. Reproduced in *Some Recollections* by Emma Hardy, it illustrates her wisdom in urging T.H. to concentrate on his writing.)

Winding its way down to Boscastle Harbour, babbling mostly to itself in its wooded valley, the Valency remains today as wild and unspoilt as when Emma and Hardy sketched, painted and picnicked along its banks more than a century ago. And even though the fugitive glass has doubtless long since disintegrated, the little waterfall with its *hollow boiling voice* endures, attesting to the percipience of a poet who never failed to recognise the wonder inherent in the less spectacular, overlooked features of landscapes noted for more magnificent arrangements.

Hence the only prime
And real love-rhyme
That I know by heart,
And that leaves no smart,
Is the purl of a little valley fall,
About three spans wide and two spans tall
Over a table of solid rock,
And into a scoop of the selfsame block;
The purl of a runlet that never ceases
In stir of kingdoms, in wars, in peaces;
With a hollow boiling voice it speaks
And has spoken since hills were turfless peaks.

BEENY CLIFF

It is with cliffs and mountains as with persons; they have what is called a presence, Hardy noted in his novel *A Pair of Blue Eyes,* adding that their power to impress *depends, as with man, upon the countenance of the cliff.* The forbidding, furrow-browed Beeny Cliff near Boscastle which Hardy first visited in Emma's company shortly after first meeting her in 1870 undoubtedly impressed the writer, although the laconic entry recording the event in his diary is terse to the point of précis – *March 10. Went with E. L. G. to Beeny Cliff. She on horseback . . . On the cliff . . . 'The tender grace of a day', etc. the run down to the edge. The coming home.* Yet over forty years later, returning and recalling in 1913 the events of *that clear-sunned March day,* he set down in the poem bearing its name his homage to the cliff and its setting. A poem concluding, as several others of that period of pilgrimages, on a note of regret for an association now saddened by loss of the one who had shared his delight in its beauty.

What if still in chasmal beauty looms that wild weird western shore,
The woman now is – elsewhere – whom the ambling pony bore,
And nor knows nor cares for Beeny, and will laugh there nevermore.

Towering seven hundred feet above the Atlantic and lying just to the east of the scene depicted is High Cliff – the *Cliff Without a Name* over which Henry Knight slipped when demonstrating to Elfride Swancourt the peculiar air currents sweeping over it in *A Pair of Blue Eyes*. Too formidable a crag for poetry perhaps, but a well-sited eminence for picnics and adventure, now cared for by the National Trust.

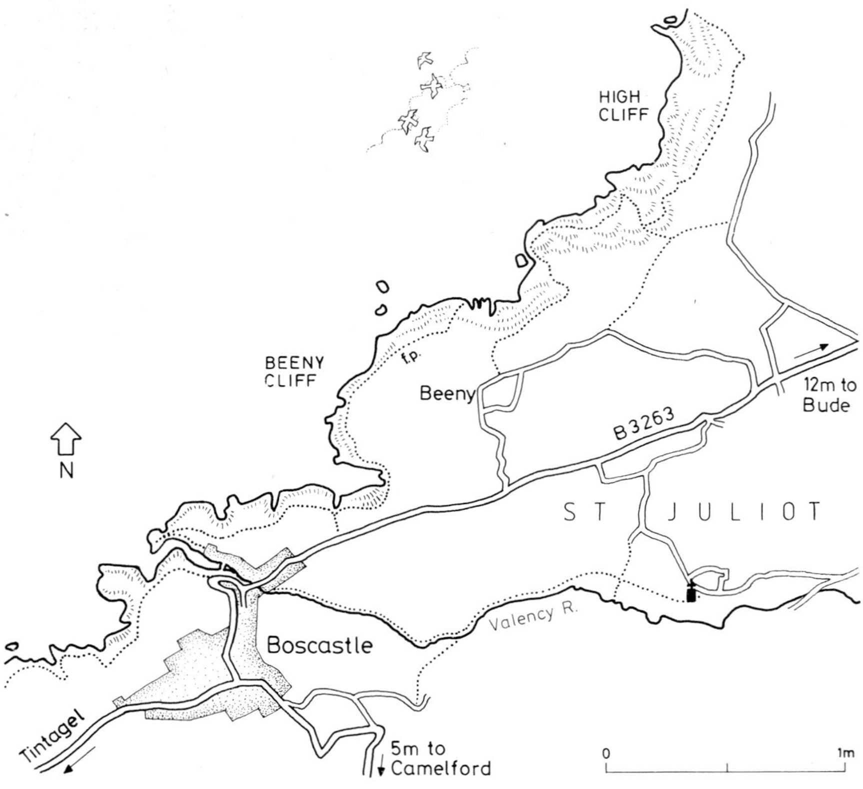

Still in all its chasmal beauty bulks old Beeny to the sky.

ST. JULIOT CHURCH

The erection of a commemorative tablet to his wife's memory in the church of St. Juliot, Cornwall, apart from being a token of the author's regard for Emma's early association with the parish, also indicates the importance he attached to the part that association played in shaping their future. For it was through accepting an architectural assignment to make a report for restoration work on the St. Juliot church that Hardy met his future wife, and although the closing years of their marriage had been marred by Emma's eccentric obsession with having married below her social station, bereavement brought the writer suddenly back across the span of forty years to the happier events of their meeting, engagement and first years together. Bridging the time gap, he made numerous pilgrimages to places that had been dear to his wife, and the experience of these journeyings with the emotions they aroused drew from him some of his finest poems – love lyrics to a departed Emma that outshone any he had written before her death. *The Marble Tablet* – opening on the quoted woeful cry – was written in September 1916 after Hardy and his second wife, Florence, had visited the St. Juliot church to see that the memorial had been installed as directed.

Of the ancient church only the original fifteenth century south aisle (now forming the nave and chancel) survived the restoration, its sturdy oak Cornish waggon roof made to seem out of place against the plain pine pews and pine roof of the restored section. And it is somewhat in keeping with the obloquy that was aimed at him as a writer that Hardy should have been held responsible by some for the architectural desecration of St. Juliot. He actually had no part in the designing of the restoration work, his rôle being to record the state of the dilapidated church with its cracked tower and rotting pew ends and to supervise the rebuilding. Several of the original sketches Hardy made of the old church remain in the safe keeping of the rector; three of them are reproduced in Emma Hardy's *Some Recollections*.

There it stands, though alas, what a little of her shows in its cold white look!

GLOUCESTER CATHEDRAL

At the end of 1911 Hardy paid a visit to Gloucester Cathedral, where in the fourteenth century the perpendicular style of English Gothic architecture originated. A wonderful example of great beauty resulting in consequence of a vile deed, the glory of Gloucester was made possible through the money that poured in to the shrine of Edward II, cruelly murdered at Berkeley Castle and buried in 1327 in what was then the Benedictine Monastery of St. Peter.

The former architect's apprentice marvelled at the grandeur of the 'new form' that had been built on the core of the old Norman church, inaugurating a style that would be perpetuated in cathedrals and churches throughout the kingdom, but was struck most by the thought that the name of the master mason who had invented this style was unknown. In the realm of much medieval architectural artistry it is the names of the administrators at the time the work was done, the abbots and bishops, who are credited, anonymity being the lot of the creative geniuses who brought it about. Hardy, as Edmund Blunden has noted, felt a personal indebtedness to those who by word or deed had lit up the general travel of mankind, and his musing on this matter inspired the poem *The Abbey Mason* that appeared the following year in *Harper's Monthly Magazine.* He dedicated it *With Memories of John Hicks, Architect,* the architect with whom he had served his apprenticeship, who had died forty-two years earlier.

The poem is a moving example of the way in which Hardy used his imagination to provide an explanation for something which could not be checked out factually, but which nevertheless leaves one thinking 'Ah yes, how well that might have been.' It certainly generates in the mind of this author the irreverent thought that only poets should be let loose to write the history books.

In Hardy's metrical account, the mason responsible for the restructuring is stymied when faced with the task of joining the transept to the nave, and this creative block leads to anguished days and fitful nights. *'You have thumped as you were working hard: I might have found me bruised and scarred,'* his wife complains one morning, and he toils long hours at the drawing board, chalking and discarding design after design and fretting that: *'Jeerers will say: "Here was a man who could not end what he began!"'* Until rising early one morning from a sleepless night he joyfully discovers that Nature has lent a hand in resolving the problem. Quite simply, freezing rain had overnight transformed his unsatisfactory chalk designs into a fine tracery pattern that he was able to translate into stone, bringing a beautiful new architectural style into being.

In the poem the abbot points out to the mason that, since the Almighty through frost and rain had provided the inspiration for his design, credit for it should only be given to God. A form of reasoning that the mason, despite the protests of his wife and fellow townsmen, humbly accepts, thus ensuring that his name is lost to posterity and just the wonder of his work remains.

– Well: when in Wessex on your rounds,
Take a brief step beyond its bounds,

And enter Gloucester: seek the quoin
Where choir and transept interjoin,

And, gazing at the forms there flung
Against the sky by one unsung –

The ogee arches transom-topped,
The tracery-stalks by spandrels stopped,

Petrified lacework – lightly lined
On ancient massiveness behind –

Muse that some minds so modest be
As to renounce fame's fairest fee,

While others boom a baseless claim,
And upon nothing rear a name.

WINCHESTER

Winchester, the ancient English capital, snugly containing within the boundary of its downland valley many interesting relics of successive waves of settlement, is a city several times mentioned in the Wessex stories and novels. It was here that a black flag slowly extending upon the breeze announced to Angel Clare and 'Liza-Lu that *the President of the Immortals had ended his sport with Tess*, and brought to a close Hardy's best-known novel. But the quotation accompanying the photograph, from his less-read collection of subtle, nobility-nobbling stories, belongs to a rather different order of narrative. It is the opening sentence of the 'Sentimental Member's' story – the writer's neat satirical comment on the waywardness of top people in which the *doubly-desired and doubly-rejected* Dorothy finally, in marriage to a respectable road contractor, finds the security *denied her by her own flesh and blood of higher degree*. And it was within the splendid edifice of the Cathedral that he found a fitting subject to wryly point a preface to his tale.

In an uninterrupted course of nearly three hundred steps eastward, he continued from the quoted sentence, *and again nearly three hundred steps westward amid those magnificent tombs, you can, for instance, compare in the most leisurely way the dry dustiness which ultimately pervades the persons of kings and bishops with the damper dustiness that is usually the final shape of commoners, curates, and others who take their last rest out of doors*. His egalitarian soul no doubt derived considerable satisfaction from this observation on the inevitable levelling process.

Among the dry dust notables the interested visitor may meditatively encounter in Winchester Cathedral are several of the Saxon kings whose powdery remains, including those of Ethelwulf, King Alfred's father, are neatly stacked away out of harm's reach in wooden mortuary chests. There is also a labelled chest for the Danish King Canute who reputedly demonstrated to the damp-footed dismay of his courtiers that his royal prerogative did not extend to the encroaching tide. A later tyrant, William Rufus, whose body was unceremoniously trundled to Winchester from the New Forest in 'a cart belonging to one Purkis', is interred beneath the floor of the Cathedral and, such is the power of evil bones, is claimed to have been the cause seven years later of the collapse of the Cathedral's original tower.

Izaak Walton, the biographer best remembered for his treatise on angling, and the novelist Jane Austen also share the shelter of Winchester's high nave. While among the notable bishops, St. Swithin, whose feast day traditionally heralds forty days and nights of either fine or foul weather, is the most famous to be honoured there. One whose damp remains were later brought into the dry, St. Swithin was a truly humble and dedicated man who expressed the wish when he died in 862 that he should be buried outside to share the elements with his parishioners. Eleven hundred years later, in 1962, his shrine in the Cathedral was rededicated in a simple modern design incorporating the several legends associated with him.

With interesting features too numerous to list within the scope of this book – a fine bronze King Alfred with sword held high, traces of William the Conqueror's palace, Winchester College (its fourteenth century founder William of Wykeham entombed in the Cathedral) – Winchester is a city well worth visiting. A place where anyone may discover for himself many of the tangible and far from fusty facets of the country's past, where the dry history book pages are vindicated and legends seem less remote.

Of all the romantic towns in Wessex, Wintoncester is probably the most convenient for meditative people to live in; since there you have a cathedral with a nave so long that it affords space in which to walk and summon your remoter moods without continually turning on your heel, or seeming to do more than take an afternoon stroll under cover from the rain or sun.

A GROUP OF NOBLE DAMES

SWANAGE

Swanage, where Hardy lived through the autumn and winter of 1875-76, lodging, as did Ethelberta, with an old sea captain while he completed the sequence of his much sought after heroine's *Comedy in Chapters*, no longer merits the snug seaside village description of a century ago. But although, as the view from the bottom joint of the Peveril Point thumb across to the curving white finger of Ballard Cliff illustrates, the town's popularity as a seaside resort and retirement area has resulted in an urban sprawl into the Purbeck palm, a certain amount of the picturesque quality of the former village remains. Beyond the piers, along the stretch of shore by the Lifeboat and Coastguard Station, fishermen continue to draw up their boats and hang out their nets; while around the motionless, duck-inhabited mill pond behind the Parish Church time lingers in a quiet atmosphere of narrow alleyways curving between weathered grey stone houses, interestingly old and unalike.

Some measure of the character of the town could be taken from its two principal though not overly conspicuous public monuments to personages neatly separated by a thousand years – Albert the Good and Alfred the Great. The latter monument, a squat column topped by four rusty cannon-balls (Russian shot pried from the hulls of British warships returned from the Crimea), commemorates Alfred's victory over the Danish fleet off Peveril Point in 877; the justifiable civic pride of association with the doughty Saxon king outweighing the slight artillery oversight of cannon-balls marking an event four centuries before the invention of gunpowder. The former monument, an even more austere arrangement of stone slabs honouring in its own way Victoria's memorially eclipsed consort, at least displays a thoughtful, more independent line in patriotic borough embellishment than the verdigris-coated, frowning Dowager Empress likenesses that terrorise squares and parks in other parts. Or at least it did until 1972 when High Street property developers dismantled it, went out of business and failed to re-erect it.

Both monuments were erected and largely paid for by John Mowlem, *The gentleman who owned half the property and had been a quarryman. Knollsea's* Horatio Alger, Mowlem at 18 left his native village on a quarry boat, landing in London with ninepence. Eventually striking out on his own, he founded the John Mowlem Construction Co. and, mainly through contracts for renewing the surface of London roads, made his fortune, returning at the age of 55 to Swanage. Improving and rebuilding most of the roads and drains in the parish, refurbishing existing and building new bridges, he erected the Institute bearing his name and 'on easy terms' sold to the parish the land to be laid out as a cemetery. Also, befitting a man of property, he brought the first constable to the village, generously contributing ten shillings a week towards his keep.

The other gentleman who owned the other half (of the property) *and had been to sea* was George Burt, Mowlem's protégé and newphew-in-law – *old Mr. B—, 'The King of Swanage'* as Hardy referred to him in his notebook when he met him in 1892. *He had a good profile, but was rougher in speech than I should have expected after his years in London – being the ordinary type of Dorset man, self-made by trade, whenever one of the county does self-make himself, which is not often.*

Promoting with Mowlem the first pier, 'old Mr. B—' in his younger days inaugurated the first boat service to Poole and Bournemouth, which in the summer season still remains a pleasant way of visiting this junior league Wessex spa.

Knollsea . . . a seaside village lying snug within two headlands as between a finger and thumb.
THE HAND OF ETHELBERTA

POOLE HARBOUR

The view afforded Ethelberta from the pad of her hired donkey as she trotted along the high ridge of Nine Barrow Down – the lofty burial ground of nine chieftains slain in a battle against the Romans – is certainly one of the most impressive panoramic views to be seen anywhere in Dorset. By arranging for his heroine to traverse this Purbeck backbone, Hardy provided himself with an opportunity to outline clearly and directly the commanding beauty of a scene in a manner especially characteristic of his writing genius, rendering in short, swift phrases an immediate impression of the visual brilliance of the view.

Mundanely translating the poetic into geographical terms, *the many-armed inland sea* is the extensive estuary forming Poole Harbour. The low, white cliffs of *Sandbourne* are faintly visible beyond the harbour entrance, at the right of the picture. And the *island with fir trees and gorse* is Brownsea Island (Brunci Insula, the Island of Bruno during the reign of Edward the Confessor) where Canute cavorted in carnal abandon with maidens he had carried off from Cerne Abbey and where, some centuries later, Lord Baden-Powell set a better example to the world by founding the Boy Scout movement and holding its inaugural camp there.

For decades tantalisingly inaccessible, the jealously guarded private domain of a well-intentioned woman whose prime concern was the welfare of the wild creatures who shared its wilderness with her, Brownsea has been administered by the National Trust since 1963. The island, with its Henry VIII castle (much modified since he built it) and derelict Maryland village (built in the middle of the last century by Colonel William Waugh, the one owner who endeavoured to make a commercial success of his purchase by establishing a pottery industry on the island), is now, with the exception of a Boy Scouts' Reserve and a Nature Sanctuary, open for exploration by all intrigued by the mystery and history contained in its 500 acres.

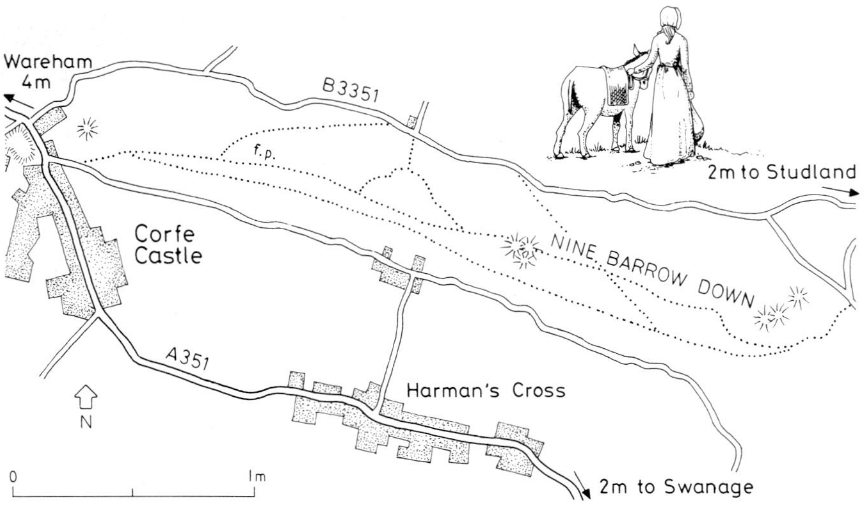

Far below . . . the silver sunbeams lighted up a many-armed inland sea which stretched round an island with fir-trees and gorse, and amid brilliant crimson heaths wherein white paths and roads occasionally met the eye in dashes and zig-zags like flashes of lightning.

THE HAND OF ETHELBERTA

CORFE CASTLE

Corfe Castle, a ruinous remnant much favoured by calendar compilers, viewed not from the familiar old world elevation embracing its village of rose-twined and awry Purbeck stone cottages and inns, but seen as it would have appeared to Ethelberta as she approached it from Nine Barrow Down.

'Ancient and grey, a dim mumbling place of tales and gossip,' was the way that Hardy's friend Treves described the village – words, with the exception of 'dim', that as well apply to the castle that dominates it. Centuries of alternating calm and conflict have endowed it with innumerable tales, and where supportable tales expire the gossip of scholarly surmise and local lay conjecture take over. King John kept his crown there, and countless wretched prisoners in its dark dungeons. Edward II was held there prior to being brutally murdered at Berkeley, Good Queen Bess undoubtedly slept there, and nobody knows for certain when it was built.

Hutchins was of the opinion that 'some circumstances will justify at least a conjecture that it was built by King Edgar', although the editors of the third edition of his *History of Dorset* doubt that anything so elaborate as a stone castle commanded the site in Saxon times and plump for William the Conqueror as builder. But, whether a castle or merely a hunting lodge was perched at *Corvsgate* at the time (the Saxon name Corf Gate indicated the pass leading into the best part of the Isle of Purbeck), all authorities are agreed that it was here in 978 that Edgar's widow, Queen Elfrida, fatally stabbed or commissioned the stabbing of Edward (the Martyr) so that her son Ethelred (the Unready) became king.

Although debate on its origin may be inconclusive, the story of how the castle was reduced to its present ruinous aspect is well-chronicled. Having withstood under the command of its royalist owner Lady Bankes (Sir John and his men were fighting alongside Charles at York) a lengthy siege by Parliamentary forces – a siege culminating in a farcical foray by 150 disorderly, well-primed sailors, brought from Poole by the lure of £20 to the first man to scale its walls and sent howling back down the slopes when showered with hot ashes by her ladyship's maids and men-servants – the castle only surrendered at the end of the second seige in February 1645 through the treachery of one of its officers infiltrating Cromwellian troops in the guise of reinforcements. In the following month a vote was taken in the Commons to 'slight' it, a few strategically placed barrels of gunpowder speedily accomplishing what Parliamentary cannon and drunken matelots had failed to achieve.

Today the Department of the Environment, sharing the cost with the National Trust to whom the castle was recently bequeathed, are constantly occupied arresting the slights of time and the English weather to maintain *the notable ruin* in much the same condition as when the demolition squad left.

The towers of the notable ruin rose out of the furthermost shoulder of the upland . . . its site being the slope and crest of a smoothly nibbled mount.

THE HAND OF ETHELBERTA

PUDDLETOWN, ST. MARY'S

Noseless and nameless, the alabaster effigy reclining on the tomb in the Athelhampton Chantry in St. Mary's Church, Puddletown is assumed to be that of fifteenth century Sir William Martyn, Knight Bachelor, (the chained creature his feet rest on not the customary dog but Martyn's ape from the family crest – an ape gazing into a mirror: 'He who looks at Martyn's ape, Martyn's ape shall look at him'). He might well have provided the inspirational take-off point for Hardy's delightful little fable on the folly of human vanity, *The Children and Sir Nameless*, for, in addition to the corresponding features already touched on, the figure stretches a good seven feet, appears to have been carved thirty years before the knight's death, and is fully equipped with the campaigning accoutrements listed in the second verse of the poem.

Poetry apart, the mainly fifteenth, part twelfth century church of St. Mary's warrants inclusion in this book for it was one of Hardy's favourite Dorset churches, a place that he often visited and with which his father's family had long been associated. Sir Frederick Treves noted: 'The feature of greatest interest in Puddletown is the Church, one of the few in the county which has been happy in escaping the hand of the restorer. No church can compare with this in human interest and nowhere can one come into closer touch with the Dorset of the past.' And certainly these were the characteristics that endeared it to Hardy, especially its fortunate survival from the former architect's particular *bête noir* – the ruthless restoration work that swept away so many valuable historic features of Wessex churches from the middle of the nineteenth century onwards.

Today St. Mary's Puddletown is still an interesting and well cared for repository of the past, housing beneath its beautiful oak-timbered roof – lovingly and painstakingly restored in 1933 – a material record of much that was good, odd and inequitable from the proceding centuries. There are the penned pews, each with its little door opening into the aisle – mute testimony to the rigid stratification pertaining in the English social system until comparatively recent times. A church document dated 1637 lists how parishioners were to be seated according to degree and rank and sexually segregated; a few frescoed texts in various states of legibility including a Cromwellian text over the south door; and, in addition to the *old stone man* illustrated, several other recumbent alabaster and Ham Hill stone Knights and Ladies, some gone a little mouldy but others still bearing on their tombs traces of original colouring.

Certainly the most historically valuable structure in this fine old church – almost the sole surviving example of what was once a regular feature of Dorset churches – is the minstrel's gallery, part of which can be glimpsed between the nameless knight and the worm-burrowed canopy that covers him. For a couple of centuries the hymns were accompanied by various combinations of musicians perched up there above the congregation, until in 1845 a barrel organ – precursor of a manual instrument – dispensed with the blowing and bowings of two clarionets, a piccolo, a bassoon and two bass-viols. Prior to 1800 and his marriage and removal to Higher Bockhampton, when he set about improving the musical arrangements in Stinsford Church (which he found to be *in a deplorable condition . . . conducted from the gallery by a solitary old man with an oboe*) Hardy's paternal grandfather – the first of three Thomas Hardys – was himself a bass-viol player in the St. Mary's gallery. Several amusing incidents relating to church minstrels that the third Thomas Hardy incorporated into his novels and stories stem from the first T.H.'s experiences, transmitted to the author by his grandmother.

Sir Nameless, once of Athelhall, declared:
"These wretched children romping in my park
Trample the herbage till the soil is bared,
And yap and yell from early morn till dark?
Go keep them harnessed to their set routines:
Thank God I've none to hasten my decay;
For green rememberance there are better means
Than offspring, who but wish their sires away."

Sir Nameless of that mansion said anon:
"To be perpetuate for my mightiness
Sculpture must image me when I am gone."
– He forthwith summoned carpenters there express
To shape a figure stretching seven-odd feet
(For he was tall) in alabaster stone,
With shield, and crest, and casque, and sword complete:
When done a statelier work was never known.

Three hundred years hied; Church-restorers came,
And, no one of his lineage being traced,
They thought an effigy so large in frame
Best fitted for the floor. There it was placed,
Under the seats for schoolchildren. And they
Kicked out his name, and hobnailed off his nose;
And, as they yawn through sermon-time, they say,
"Who was this old stone man beneath our toes?"

CLYFFE HILL CLUMP

The pessimist label is a tag that Hardy for his pains was and frequently still is lumbered with, simply because he endeavoured to present the world as he truly saw it, a place in which mortals strive towards unattainable ends, often happily but always hopelessly, against the weighted scales of an enigmatic divine ordering. And nowhere is his unblinkered view of the universe more succinctly and uncompromisingly expressed than in his short, sharp poem *Yell'ham-Woods Story*.

It says that Life would signify
A thwarted purposing:
That we come to live, and are called to die.

Pessimism? Or just plain realism?

Perched high on their hill overlooking Southover Heath near Tolpuddle in the heart of Dorset, a commanding landmark for miles around moaning affirmation as the wind tugs at their topknots, the ragged regiment of Clyffe Hill Clump has been considerably depleted since Hardy wrote the poem. Yet, forlornly thinned by the elements, their bare and broken outlines emphasise more vividly now the pungency of his closing line – sombre but uncontestable – *'Life offers – to deny!'*

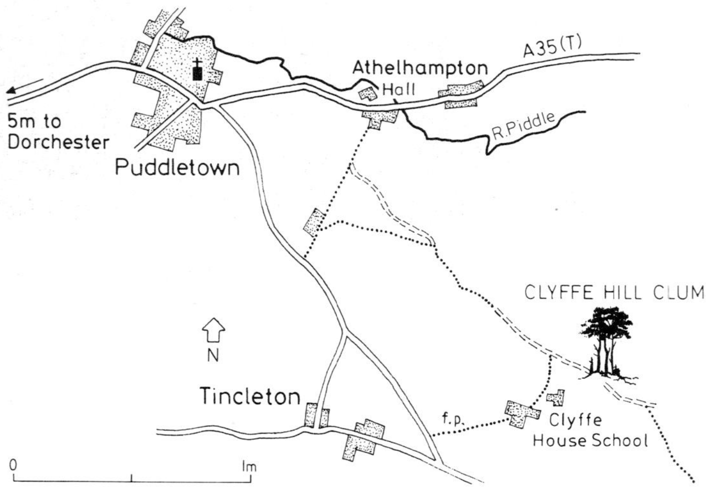

COOMB-FIRTREES say that Life is a moan
And Clyffe-hill Clump says "Yea!"

'LITTLE HINTOCK'

The *Little Hintock* hamlet where many of the events in what was in several respects Hardy's best and most informative novel took place had no definite real life counterpart. It was a composite creation of the author's in which he drew on features taken from various places lying within the woodland scene he was writing about – the stretch of country crowned by the lofty eminence of High Stoy where the uplands descend into the Vale of Blackmoor – to fashion a fictional hamlet which he peopled with such believable characters as Giles Winterborne, Marty South and her unfortunate father John with his phobia about the large tree growing outside his cottage and threatening his life.

Yet so well had he delineated the hamlet, many readers when the book first appeared in 1887 felt sure that *Little Hintock* was merely a literary disguise, and many others after roaming the area were certain that they had found its original. The humour of this did not escape Hardy. In writing the preface to the later Wessex edition of this novel, the writer, with tongue well in cheek, referring to the enquiries he had had regarding the hamlet's true name and exact locality, mentioned that to oblige readers he had once spent several hours on a bicycle with a friend in an attempt to discover the real spot – *but the search ended in failure; though tourists assure me positively that they have found it without trouble.*

Hardy knew, of course, even at the time of writing *The Woodlanders* that the occupational way of life he was describing in its pages was steadily changing, and today much that was woodland is treeless, arable land. But the hamlets and villages remain substantially as they were when the novel was written. Tucked away at the end of a little road that leads to nowhere else, Melbury Osmond has been chosen as most aptly matching the *Little Hintock* quotation. Hardy took the name Melbury for that of his heroine Grace's family, and the small village was one that he knew intimately; it had a strong association with his own family, his mother having been born there.

In centuries past the village must have been an industrious little community, the Dorset historian Hutchins noting that it once carried on 'an extensive trade in horn buttons and plated buckles.' Dowlas, a strong unbleached linen cloth used extensively in the sixteenth century, was also manufactured there. But now, with just a couple of small farms its only claim to commerce, Melbury Osmond is a village in retirement, content to contemplate the shadows slowly moving around its stone and thatch cottages as it savours the tranquility afforded by its secluded setting in a fold of the hills.

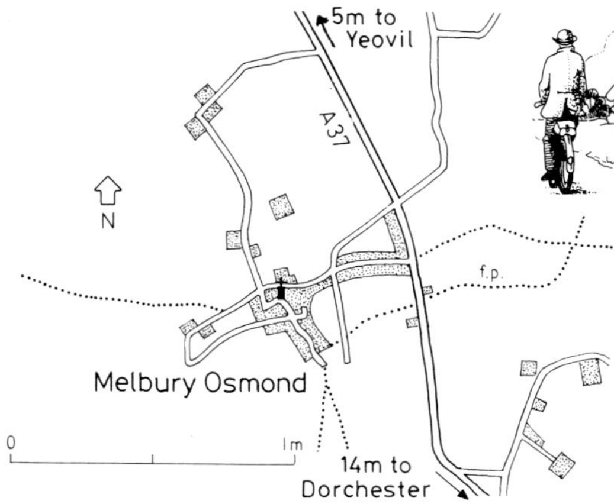

One of those sequestered spots outside the gates of the world where usually may be found more meditation than action, and more listlessness than meditation.

THE WOODLANDERS

OXFORD

As a guide to his readers, Hardy drew for inclusion in the later editions of his novels a map of their Wessex settings, and on the upper reaches of the Thames, marking the northernmost limit of this reconstituted kingdom, indicated the city of *Christminster*. Geographically it coincides with Oxford, although least of all the places used in his writing was this meant to be seen other than a purely arbitrary positioning. Essentially Hardy's conception of *Christminster* was a city of the mind representing the search for knowledge and truth in a shifting and uncertain world; and nowhere is the ethereal quality of the city so well evoked as in the early passage of his ultimate novel where the boy Jude experiences his first distant glimpse of its shining spires and domes through the thinning mist *either directly seen, or miraged in the peculiar atmosphere*. But the dream had eventually to give way to reality for Jude as well as for his creator, and as a general model for the earthly city Hardy, the former architect, with an eye for the beauty of its buildings and surroundings, selected the ancient university city of Oxford.

Following the author's directions, one can picture Jude, still haunted by his early unrealised aspirations, standing in the rain with his sad little family by the Church of St. Mary the Virgin in front of Wren's theatre, the Radcliffe Camera, and discoursing on the world's appraisal of failure and success as they watched the assembling red-robed Doctors arriving for the Encaenia – the annual ceremony commemorating the benefactors of the University. And it was in the Sheldonian Theatre behind the Radcliffe Camera, a quarter of a century after publication of the novel that was to draw such violent attacks from the critics and other quarters (*After these verdicts from the press its next misfortune was to be burnt by a bishop – probably in his despair at not being able to burn me*) as to decide its author to make it his final one (*A man must be a fool to deliberately stand up to be shot at*), Hardy was accorded academic recognition of his own success by being invested with the honorary degree of Doctor of Letters.

'Scilicet ut Virgilio nostro sic huic quoque "molle atque facetum adnuerunt gaudentes rure Camenae" – Surely as with Virgil, so with him, have the Muses that rejoice in the countryside approved his smoothness and elegance,' were the words with which the Public Orator commenced his presentation address. It was an observation that the supporting Pan at the top-left of the picture might well have piped assent to.

They turned in on the left by the church with the Italian porch, . . . till there arose on Jude's sight the circular theatre with that well-known lantern above it, which stood in his mind as the sad symbol of his abandoned hopes.

JUDE THE OBSCURE

WOOL

Whenever he could do so, Hardy delighted in restoring the earlier names to places that he selected as the settings for his stories and novels. It served, among other things, to emphasise the long-settled tradition of the regions in which the dramas affecting the lives of his latter-day West Saxons took place. *Wellbridge*, where Tess and Angel spent their ill-fated honeymoon, might now be called Woolbridge, or merely Wool; but the name Welle (probably deriving, as Hutchins notes in his *History of Dorset,* from the springs that abound in the area) can be traced as far back as the Domesday Book, and in the reign of Edward III repairs necessary to the bridge of 'Wellebrigge' are recorded.

Hardy was conscious also of the wealth of orally transmitted legends supplementing the written record in the country areas, often incorporating them to give colour to his narratives. The legend of the d'Urberville Coach, referred to by Angel Clare when Tess expresses her nervous apprehension regarding the carriage in which they drive off from their wedding, derived from a local tradition concerning a once flesh and blood Turberville. Some three centuries ago, a tempestuous member of this ancient Dorset family abducted a young heiress in the family coach; since when anyone having a trace of Turbeville blood in his veins passing over the stone bridge on the anniversary night of this event is vouchsafed a sight of the spectral coach and hears the screams of the abducted maiden. An old countryman told Hardy how he had once been forced to stand back in one of the recesses of the bridge to permit the coach to pass, and that it was like a cold mist striking him.

On the far side of the bridge, Woolbridge Manor, reduced to the status of a farmhouse at the time of *Tess*, has in more recent times been a hotel. It is now once more a private residence, retaining within its solid stone walls the mellow charms of its literary and historic associations.

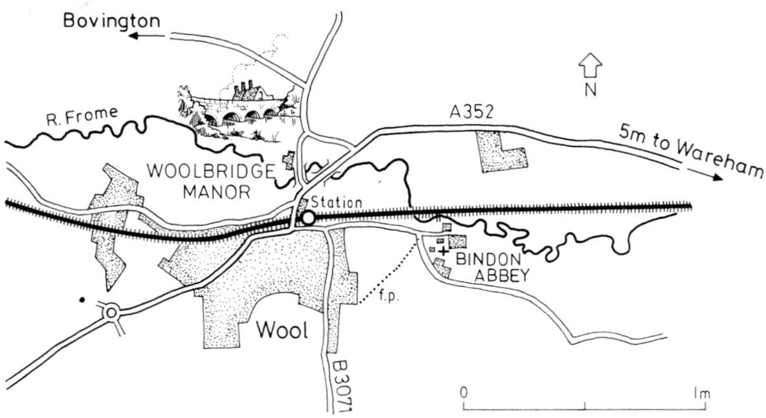

They drove over the great Elizabethan bridge which gives the place half its name.

TESS OF THE D'URBERVILLES

WOOLBRIDGE MANOR

The alarming ladies at the top of the stairs that gave Tess such a fright on first arriving at *Wellbridge Manor, owing to their being builded into the wall,* still remain to *haunt the beholder afterwards in his dreams,* although the originals admittedly have a less startling impact now than they had at the time the novel was published. Then, although having been painted directly onto the panels a couple of centuries before, their features were quite distinct and terrifying, just as Hardy described them. Ironically though, drawing attention to these long-neglected 'masterpieces' proved a sad disservice to their ferocious mien.

Suddenly made aware of the paintings' importance, the owners set about making the dark but distinct features clearer, and soon, by injudicious applications of soap and water, had accomplished what the years had failed to achieve – rendered them faint and hardly distinguishable. Fortunately for posterity, to keep them clear in his mind while writing about them, Hardy had previously made some rough pencil sketches of the 'Dames', and at a later date an unknown artist (possibly his sister Mary, who was a talented amateur portrait painter), working from these sketches, painted full-sized water colours which were presented to him. It is these paintings, donated by Florence Hardy to the Dorset County Museum after his death and now hanging in the Hardy Room there, that are featured in the photographs.

But who were these immortalised ogresses, these fugitives from femininity? *'I have been told by old folk that they were ladies of the d'Urberville family',* the charwoman informed Angel Clare, and it's likely enough that the gruesome twosome were in fact Turbervilles long descended from Sir Pagan (or Payne de) Turberville who crossed over with William the Conqueror and who assisted William Rufus in his conquest of Glamorganshire. Hutchins, the eighteenth century historian whose *History of Dorset* served Hardy both as source-book and inspirational spring-board, records that the family first established itself in Dorset at Bere Regis during the reign of Henry III, other branches later being located at Winterborne Whitchurch and Woolbridge.

. . . women of middle age, of a date some two hundred years ago, whose lineaments once seen can never be forgotten.

The long pointed features, narrow eye, and smirk of the one, so suggestive of merciless treachery;

the bill-hook nose, large teeth, and bold eye of the other, suggesting arrogance to the point of ferocity, haunt the beholder afterwards in his dreams.

TESS OF THE D'URBERVILLES

BINDON ABBEY

The ludicrous episode in *Tess* where her somnambulistic spouse Angel Clare, muttering 'Dead, dead, dead,' carries his woken wife wrapped in a sheet along the chill banks of the Frome, across a narrow plank bridge and into the grounds of Bindon Abbey may not have seemed so laughable when it was written. To a magazine-reading public, the incident that culminates with Clare placing her in the abbot's coffin and stretching out beside her on the damp grass was a measure of the melodrama the Victorians expected from their fiction. However, it enabled Hardy to bring yet another odd and obsure item of Wessex antiquity to his reader's attention.

Founded in 1172, the Cistercian abbey at Bindon was a magnificent edifice in a tranquil setting, sheltered by beeches, with an extensive system of water courses and fishponds in the grounds to ensure a constant supply of fresh fish for the refectory. The monks also had free warren to hunt and preserve game on the vast estates that accrued to the abbey through bequests. By all accounts they were not a mean lot, though, and had a reputation for generosity. At one o'clock each day, for example, a bell would be rung and men working in the fields, or anyone for that matter who heard it, could join the monks at table with no questions asked and nothing to pay on the way out.

Generosity notwithstanding, however, the abbey was soon demolished after the Dissolution, Henry VIII carting away a lot of the stone to help build Sandsfoot and Portland Castles. Traces of the carved stone can also be found built into the walls of cottages in nearby villages, but the looting was not confined to the secular. Tradition has it that the abbey's twelve bells were taken and hung in Wool, Combe Keynes and Fordington churches, giving rise to the doggerel

'Wool streams and Combe wells,
Fordington cuckolds stole Bindon Bells.'

Thomas Poynings, first Viscount Bindon, to whom the vast estates were granted, built a manor on the monastery site, but this burnt down in 1644 shortly after the land had been sold to Humphrey Weld. Bindon was now back in Catholic hands, the Weld family having remained true to the faith throughout the years. Even so, this didn't inhibit them from removing the bulk of what was left of the ruins to build Lulworth Castle, which itself was severely damaged by fire in 1929. Divine disapproval of the desecration, perhaps?

The Welds, who included a cardinal in their lineage, were nevertheless devout and at the end of the eighteenth century built a chapel on what was probably the site of the abbot's dwelling – 'Bindon Abbey' house in the picture. For a period at the end of the last century the rooms on the ground floor were used as a Roman Catholic school.

The empty stone coffin, a watery grave in the early autumn photograph, is reputedly that of Abbot Richard de Maners (circa 1310), a stone cover that had once had a brass indent of the abbot having been found nearby. There's no knowing how his rest was disturbed, although after the Dissolution the water courses were extended, when the cemetery on the north side of the abbey church was cut into and skeletons and coffins dug up. The diggers were surprised to discover that, rather like Western frontiersmen, the monks were buried with their boots on.

The ruined site is still part of the Weld estate. It is not accessible to the public, 'Bindon Abbey' house being now a private residence. When I made arrangements with the present tenant to take the photograph, however, he told me that in the tourist season there are still the occasional macabre-minded callers asking permission to stretch out in the coffin. At least it's an indication that Hardy's *Tess* is still being read.

Against the north wall was the empty stone coffin of an abbot, in which every tourist with a turn for grim humour was accustomed to stretch himself.

TESS OF THE D'URBERVILLES

MARNHULL

Though occasionally the Wessex name that Hardy constructed for a place confused those of his many readers who liked to link it with its real life counterpart, few can have failed to identify immediately the village he selected as the birthplace for his eponymous heroine, Tess. *Marlott . . . amid the north-eastern undulations of the beautiful Vale of Blakemore or Blackmoor* acknowledges the earlier name for Marnhull, namely Marlhill; a name derived from the deposits of white clay or marl that crop up in the region, hardening to freestone after exposure to the air.

Inevitably with the passage of years there have been changes, particularly in respect to the growth of this prosperous rural community. Yet even so, the turnpike keeper's reply to Tess's enquiry when she returned home after parting from Angel Clare is nevertheless quite apt. Were Hardy to return now, for example, to the short crooked lane in which he found the cottage he chose as Tess's home, he would find the cottage and its setting substantially as when he wrote about it. And though new dwellings fill the empty spaces in this *long and broken village*, at the quiet centre featured in the photograph Marlott is certainly Marlott still.

The fifteenth century tower of St. Gregory's church remains the dominating landmark of John Leland's 'good uplandishe town.' Outwardly little has changed, though one would look in vain now in the trim and tidy churchyard for *that corner of God's allotment where He lets the nettles grow* – the unconsecrated corner where Tess buried her baby, Sorrow the Undesired who had been blessed only by her own hastily extemporised baptismal service.

It is across the road from the church at the Crown Inn where the firmest link with Hardy's novel is established now. Here, in the convivial atmosphere of the pleasant flagstone-floored Pure Drop public bar with its large old fireplace and horse-shoe shaped bar, one can readily summon up the beery ghost of Tess's lovable, feckless father 'Sir John' Durbeyfield holding boastful court amongst his less 'noble' fellow locals.

Hardy's friend Hermann Lea noted that Marnhull was once known as 'the booziest place in Dorset.' Since at the time Hardy wrote the novel the village maintained no less than two breweries and a malthouse, its reputation was doubtless well founded and may have influenced the writer in his choice of locale for old Durbeyfield. One won't exactly find rustics reeling in the ditches there nowadays, of course. However, hanging in the Pure Drop Bar there is a framed pencil cartoon that I judge to date from one of the 'drought' periods of the last war or a year or two afterwards. Strategically ranged round the pub entrances, crouched behind empty barrels and suchlike, the Pure Drop regulars are levelling their shotguns at a party of thirsty 'furriners' approaching up the hill towards them. The caption – 'Remember men, if you want the beer to last out until next week, make every shot count.' Marlott, one can't help feeling, may well to some degree besides its little changed physical aspect, be Marlott still.

'Marlott is Marlott still'

TESS OF THE D'URBERVILLES

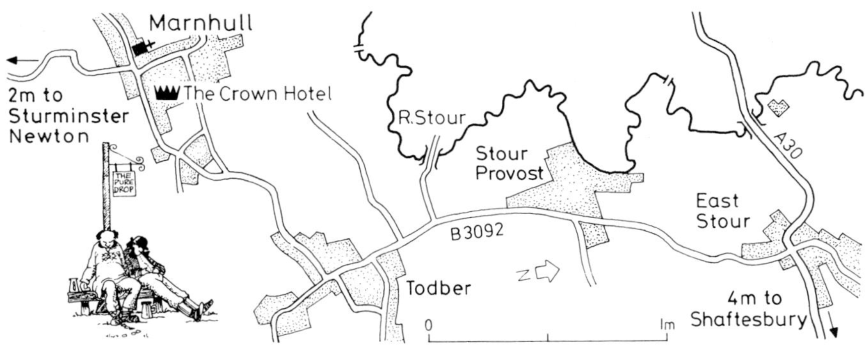

WIMBORNE MINSTER QUARTER JACK

Regularly since 1613, the *jack-o'-clock* or Quarter Jack, standing between his two bells high up outside a window on the north wall of the west tower of Wimborne Minster, has with mechanical precision rung the passing quarter hours and provided the inhabitants of this interesting old market town with a reliable check for their clocks and watches. Originally he was attired more befittingly but less colourfully as a monk, although from Napoleonic times he has appeared in the bright garb of a Grenadier, and it is the little time-keeper's military mien that Hardy has rhythmically evoked with the tempo of his poem *Copying Architecture in an Old Minster.* In part expressing the poet's keen awareness of time passing, the poem is one of several he wrote about Wimborne – the *Warborne* of *Two on a Tower – where they draw up young gam'sters' brains like rhubarb under a nine-penny pan*, and where the Hardys lived for a couple of years before moving to Dorchester.

It's a poetical sort of place in a cow-contented meadowland setting where the rivers Allen and Stour meet, with narrow twisting streets and humpy little bridges. Here, in 871, Alfred the Great came to bury his elder brother Ethelred the Martyr, slain in combat with the Danes who later destroyed the Abbey church he was buried in. A brass set in a Purbeck marble slab in the Minster erected on the site about a century afterwards records the nature of his death but misdates it by a couple of years.

Less conspicuous than the 'Man in the Window', but an equally odd fellow, is 'The Man in the Wall.' This is a tomb in the Trinity Chapel containing the remains of Anthony Ettricke, the magistrate before whom, after his capture on nearby Horton Heath, the Duke of Monmouth was taken. Ettricke, offended by the people of Wimborne, perhaps for his rôle in sealing the captured Duke's doom (Monmouth's cause was strongly supported locally) vowed that he would not be buried in the Minster nor without it, neither in its ground, nor above it. Later, however, wishing to be buried near his ancestors, he contrived to keep to the letter of his vow by arranging to have his coffin placed during his lifetime within a niche in the wall and inscribed with the date 1693. He was ten years out in his reckoning and actually died in 1703, the year being oddly overinscribed on his emblazoned coffin.

But although a certain quaint carelessness with dates may be characteristic of the old Minster, the recording of time is a notable feature of the church for, in addition to the Quarter Jack, operated by a separate mechanism that strikes the hours on a tenor bell in the belfry, there is the great-grandfather clock of Dorset that was built by a Glastonbury monk in 1320. Predating our proper concept of the cosmos by a couple of centuries, it is an unusual orrery depicting the sun (marking the hours) and the moon (revolving on its axis to indicate its phases) revolving concentrically around a stationary earth. There are only three others of this type known to be still in existence, all in the West Country – at Wells Cathedral, Exeter Cathedral and Ottery St. Mary.

How smartly the quarters of the hour march by
That the jack-o'-clock never forgets;
. . . .
Just so did he clang here before I came,
And so will he clang when I'm gone.

WIMBORNE MINSTER CHURCHYARD

Country churchyards, a constant source of inspiration for poets, evoked in Hardy responses not always of the most expected kind. Not that he was incapable of such thoughts as expressed in Gray's memorable 'Elegy'; he certainly was, but his keen observation and insatiable curiosity often attracted him to the more bizarre and even ludicrous aspects of the ultimate in earthly depositories. As a young architectural assistant he had once, when the Midland Railway was to put a cutting through old St. Pancras Churchyard, been given the task of supervising, at night, the exhumation and removal of the coffins, being particularly surprised when one rotted coffin on falling apart disclosed a skeleton and two skulls. And old country churchyards with their fading stone pages, he later realised, had individual characteristics he could incorporate into his writing to suite a mood, strike a symbolic parallel, or, as in the poem *The Levelled Churchyard* here quoted in its entirety, merely give vent to his finely developed sense of the ridiculous.

The poem was written in 1882 while the Hardys were living in the Dorset market town of Wimborne (the house they were living in, Laherne in Avenue Road, now sports a blue plaque). The Wimborne Minster authorities at that time, in the interest of easier mowing and to provide a clear greensward to set off the Minster, had uprooted the old gravestones. Many of the durable old memorials came in handy for replacing broken paving leading up to this fine old church and for flagging the porches, whilst others were laid out flat at grass level, causing confusion in heaven perhaps, but a certain tidiness in the Minster precincts. The photograph is a view at the south side of the church which is featured in another Hardy poem, *Copying Architecture in an Old Minster,* quoted and illustrated on the previous page.

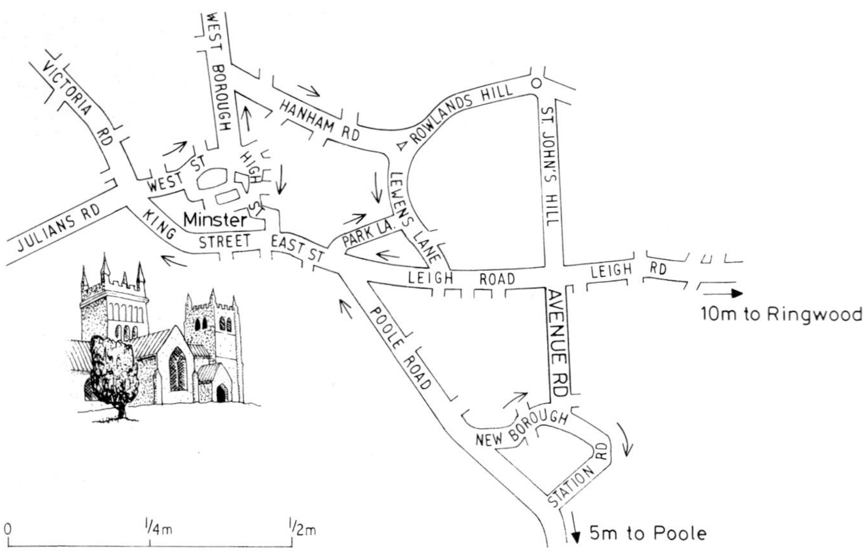

'O Passenger, pray list and catch
  Our sighs and piteous groans,
Half stifled in this jumbled patch
  Of wrenched memorial stones!

'We late-lamented, resting here,
  Are mixed to human jam,
And each to each exclaims in fear,
  'I know not which I am!

'The wicked people have annexed
  The verses on the good;
A roaring drunkard sports the text
  Teetotal Tommy should!

'Where we are huddled none can trace,
  And if our names remain,
They pave some path or porch or place
  Where we have never lain!

'Here's not a modest maiden elf
  But dreads the final Trumpet,
Lest half of her should rise herself,
  And half some sturdy strumpet!

'From restorations of Thy fane,
  From smoothings of thy sward,
From zealous Churchmen's pick and plane
  Deliver us O Lord! Amen!'

HORTON INN

Lonely old country inns with the romantic atmosphere that such places evoke had a particular attraction for Hardy, and many remote Wessex taverns, either under their own or a slightly disguised sign, found their way into his work. Part of *A Tramp-woman's Tragedy*, for example, the poem he considered to be his most successful, reads as a regular roll-call of several such hostelries.

Lone inns we loved my man and I,
My man and I;
'King's Stag', 'Windwhistle' high and dry,
'The Horse' on Hintock Green,
The cosy house at Wynyard's Gap,
'The Hut' renowned on Bredy Knap,
And many another wayside tap
Where folk might sit unseen.

Horton Inn, to restore the proper name of the pub Hardy had in mind as the rendezvous for his eloping heroine in the Old Surgeon's macabre and brutal story in the *Noble Dames* collection, is still almost as solitary as it was two hundred years or so ago. The former old coaching inn built somewhere about the time of Queen Anne, standing by itself at an unimportant cross-roads on the Wimborne/Cranborne road, looks out onto a countryside with a wealth of historical associations. It is country over which King John hunted, and also where another with a claim to the English throne was himself hunted and captured.

Just about two miles from where the inn stands the wretched Duke of Monmouth, whose ill-fated Wessex-raised rebellion and its consequences particularly interested Hardy, was betrayed by an old countrywoman after having travelled many weary miles from the battlefield at Sedgemoor with the hope of escaping back to France. This was at Monmouth's Ash Farm along Lousy Lane. 'May you die lousy, madam' the young Duke is reputed to have flung back at Amy Farrant, who had disclosed his hiding place and who gleefully railed at him when the militia brought him past her cottage. She did, ostracised by the whole community. The trunk of an ash growing from the bole of the original tree above the ditch he was hiding in bears a small plaque recording the sad event.

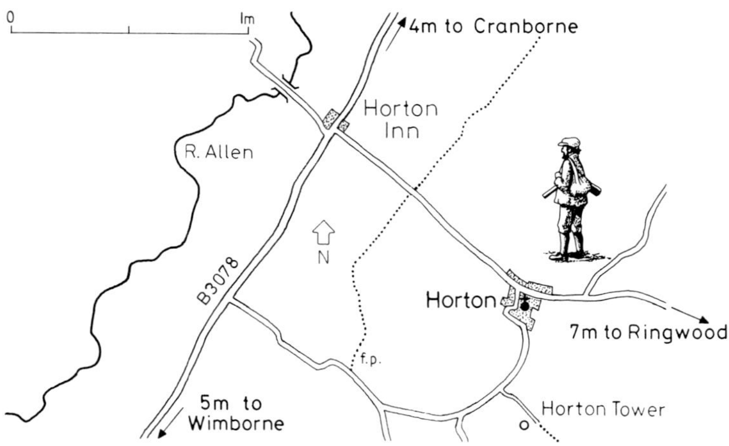

. . . the solitary wayside tavern called Lornton Inn – the rendezvous of many a daring poacher for operations in the adjoining forest.

A GROUP OF NOBLE DAMES

CHARBOROUGH TOWER and WEATHERBY CASTLE

Wessex being a region randomly dotted with towering 'follies', Hardy was well supplied with models to fashion the makeshift astronomer's tower on which his *slightly-built romance* setting *the emotional history of two infinitesimal lives against the stupendous background of the stellar universe* is pivotted. Displaying a typical catholicity in his selection, he picked on two columns rising to the west of Wimborne (the *Warborne* of the novel) where he was living while serially penning *Two On A Tower* for the *Atlantic Monthly*, merging features from both sites and the surrounding countryside into the *mise en scène* of the story.

Of the two towers, only that shown in the upper photograph – Charborough Tower near Sturminster Marshall – could have been climbed by Swithin St. Cleve for his study of the stars and planets. Built as a landscape improver by Edward Drax in 1790, it has been described as an example of 'the most distinctive and aggressive Strawberry Hill Gothic', (Sir Frederick Treves in his *Highways and Byways in Dorset*). Struck by lightning in 1838, it was 'unfortunately re-erected (Treves again) in the following year to a height upwards of a hundred feet – forty feet higher than the original. Although still a notable landmark likely to dominate the scene for some time yet, crumbling decay has set in and it is no longer considered safe to climb to its summit for the *pleasurable effect . . . to be derived from looking into four counties.*

The structure in the lower photograph – solid brick surmounted by a stone sphere – belongs more to the order of obelisks. Built atop Weatherby Castle, an early British earthwork surrounded by farm land, its physical location is that described for the Rings-Hill Speer of the story. Yet no landmark this, for although when built it doubtless could be seen for miles, aspiring trees and clambering creepers now challenge its dominance and a full view of its tapering shaft can only be obtained from its base.

To fit the requirements of his novel Hardy selected 1782 as the year of the tower's erection; its purpose being a memorial to Lord Constantine's great-grandfather, *a respectable officer who had fallen in the American War.* A stone tablet over the door bearing some inscription to this effect was no longer readable, having been *smoothed over by a plaster of lichen.*

Here stood this aspiring piece of masonry, erected as the most conspicuous and ineffaceable reminder of a man that could be though of; and yet the whole aspect of the memorial betokened forgetfulness. Probably not a dozen people within the district knew the name of the person commemorated, while perhaps not a soul remembered whether the column were hollow or solid, whether with or without a tablet explaining its date and purpose.

The Weatherby Castle column, also a memorial to one man, likewise shares the oblivion accorded the Rings-Hill Speer monument. Its stone tablet, intelligible but brief, reads: 1716 E.M.P. Few but the local historian know that it stands neglected on the forgotten earthwork to honour Edmund Morton Pleydell, a squire from nearby Milborne St Andrew who died, not heroically in some corner of a foreign field, but peacefully in his bed.

. . . the pillar rose into the sky a bright and cheerful thing, unimpeded, clean and flushed with the sunlight.

TWO ON A TOWER

WINTERBORNE TOMSON

The period when Hardy was launching into his first career as an architect was one in which church restoration work was at its peak, and many fine and interesting features in centuries-old buildings were swept away by over-zealous and tidy-minded mid-Victorians with good intentions but a poor sense of preservation. Recalling this period years later in a paper written for the Society of Antiquaries, Hardy, ever conscious of the rich human associations of ancient buildings, ruefully remarked on the irremediable damage done, but at the same time noted the conflict that is always present in restoration work between *wanting to retain the old while at the same time recreating and saving from the annihilating hand of time. The opposing tendencies excited in an architect by the distracting situation can find no satisfactory reconciliation. All that he can do is of the nature of compromise.*

Looking back across the years, Hardy was also able to appreciate the wry humour of events which at the time they occured must have occasioned him acute embarrassment to say the least. At one church restoration he had been supervising he was shocked on arriving at the church to find that a fine old window had been knocked out and a *caricature in new stone of the old window had taken its place.* The contractor proudly explained that, not wishing to spoil the ship for a ha'porth of tar, he had got rid of the old 'winder' and put a new one in its place, all on his own generous account. On another occasion, on the same job, Hardy had been horrified to find that an old oak rood screen had, without authorisation, been replaced by a shiny new deal one. To his anxious enquiry concerning the whereabouts of the old one, the contractor blithely replied: *'Used up to boil the workmen's kittles; though 'a were not much at that!'*

To do nothing, where to act on little knowledge is a dangerous thing, is to do most and best, Hardy wrote of those churchmen who had been guided by a policy of *masterly inaction* and simply left their historic buildings alone. There are instances, though, where 'to do nothing' may mean the total loss of some historically valuable old building. To prevent such losses the Society for the Protection of Ancient Buildings was founded, and it is one of the most pleasantly

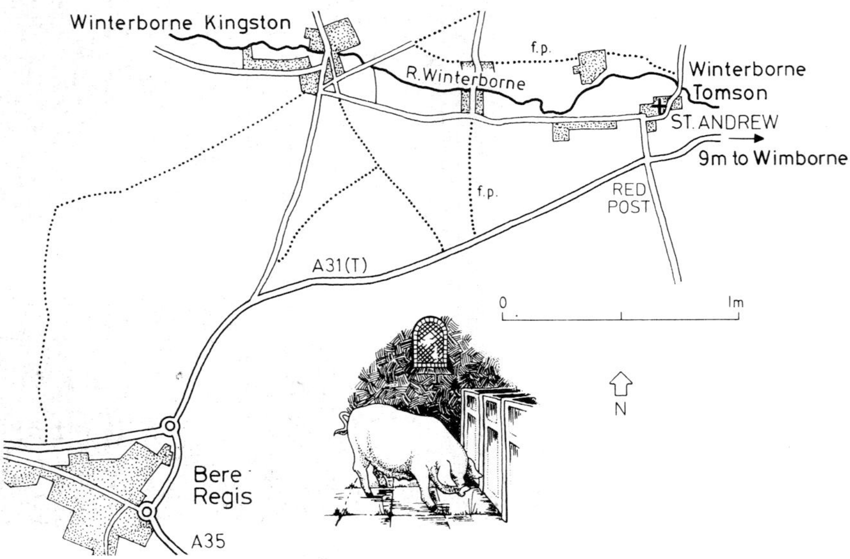

The human interest in an edifice ranks before its architectural interest, . . . Life, after all, is more than art, and that which appealed to us in the (maybe) clumsy outlines of some structure which had been looked at and entered by a dozen generations of ancestors outweighs the more subtle recognition, if any, of architectural qualities.

MEMORIES OF CHURCH RESTORATION

apt features of Thomas Hardy's career that his paper, *Memories of Church Restoration*, should after his death have been instrumental in saving from ruin a small, simple but architecturally unique ancient Dorset church.

The church of St. Andrew, Winterborne Tomson, built of flint and stone eight centuries ago by the Normans, with its medieval waggon roof shaped into the rounded apse, small minstrel's gallery and high box-pews, had for generations served the spiritual needs of the little community, until in the last century the village departed, leaving it isolated and deserted. Pigs from the nearby farmyard inquisitively rooted among the weeds growing up between the flagstones in the aisle, the windows were broken, birds nested in the ancient high pews. And so it remained for over fifty years, derelict and decaying, until the attention of the S.P.A.B. was drawn to the plight of this little architectural gem. Under the leadership of Albert Reginal Powys, architect brother of the talented Wessex family that included the writers John Cowper, Llewelyn and Theodore Francis, the Society looked into the matter and the need for preservation was readily recognised. A. R. Powys carried out the survey himself and plans were drawn up to restore the church to the state in which it had existed more than half a century previously when the parishioners left it after the last service. But the long years of total neglect had taken their toll and the estimated cost of the work to be undertaken was such as would have strained the slender resources of the Society beyond limit. Then, providentially, the original MS of Hardy's paper was discovered in the S.P.A.B. archives, and the sale of this together with other MSS a year after the writer's death raised £1,000 – sufficient faithfully and lovingly to restore the small edifice.

Rededicated, the little church is once more a place of worship; in its sturdy, honest simplicity a tangible testimony to qualities shared alike by the two men whose work ensured its survival.

HARDY'S TOMB

It had always been Hardy's wish, when at last it should be time to lay down his pen, to be laid to rest in the little churchyard of St. Michael's Stinsford. Not only was it the place where his wife Emma, his parents and his grandparents were buried, but the peaceful little hamlet of Stinsford bordering the lush Frome meadows had formed the background against which many of his poems and stories had been set. There could be no better last biding place for one who cared as much as he did for the country ways, follies and foibles, joys and sadnesses, strengths and weaknesses of folk such as he lovingly immortalised in his legendary Mellstock Quire; and there with Dewy and Reuben under the gaunt yew tree, when he could no longer write about them, he wished to remain.

However, between writing *Under the Greenwood Tree*, and his death more than half a century later, Thomas Hardy's name had become a household word. He was world-renowned as a writer and burial in an obscure country plot ran counter to the prevailing national sentiment. It was the nation's wish that the man who, ironically, less than four years before he died had written in his poem *A Refusal:*

Said the grave Dean of Westminster:
'Mine is the best minster . . .
So therefore I cannot
Rule here if I ban not
Such liberty-taking
As movements for making
Its grayness environ
The memory of Byron . . .
'Twill next be expected
That I get erected
To Shelley a tablet . . .
Then – what makes my skin burn,
Yea, forehead to chin burn –
That I ensconce Swinburne!'

should himself be enshrined in that edifice –

Whose dict is but Christian
Though nicknamed Philistian.

How then to reconcile the two wishes? Compromise, that sturdy English characteristic that has been responsible for more odd arrangements than any other form of policy guide, settled for the surgical removal of the writer's heart prior to the incineration of his body and ceremonial installing of his ashes in Poets' Corner. Then, at a small ceremony at Stinsford, a casket containing his heart – reputed seat of the emotions – was lowered into the opened grave of Emma Hardy, there to be joined nine years later by the body of his second wife Florence. Not everyone was happy with this arrangement, but at least honour, or rather honouring appeared to have been satisfied by this dissective process and his heart was in the right place. Or was it?

A local tradition maintains that in fact the casket lowered alongside Emma's coffin did not contain the writer's heart, that earlier, while workmen were attending to the final arrangements for the ceremony, the casket had been left unattended and a sly, curious cat had pawed up the cover, dabbed out the heart and eaten it! However unfounded the legend may be – it has been authoritatively denied by Hardy's cook who claimed the surgeon used one of her best cake tins to put the heart in after the operation – the fanciful picture would certainly have been appreciated by Hardy. If his indisseverable shade still lingers in the Wessex twilight he is sure to have popped the tale into his notebook.

There Dewy lay by the gaunt yew tree,
There Reuben and Michael a pace behind
And Bowman with his family
By the wall that the ivies bind.

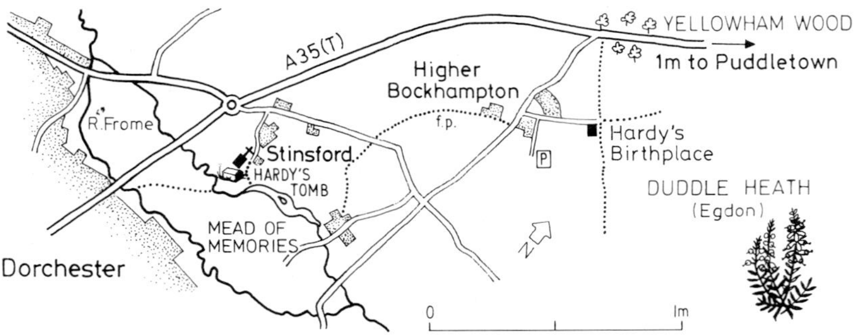

CHRONOLOGY

1840 Thomas Hardy was born on June 2nd at Higher Bockhampton, Stinsford, Dorset, the first son of four children of Thomas Hardy, a stone mason, and Jemima Hardy. Of small physique, he was thrown aside as dead by the surgeon attending his birth.

1848 Considered strong enough by his parents at eight to attend the village school where he excels in arithmetic and geography.

1849 Moves to the old British School in the county town of Dorchester where he distinguishes himself in Latin and has thoughts about entering the Church.

1856 Hardy becomes a pupil of John Hicks, an architect in Dorchester, though continuing his Latin studies and taking up Greek. He is able to turn for help in this to the Dorset poet and philologist William Barnes who has a school next door.

1862 Moves to London where he works for the next five years with Sir Arthur Blomfield, winning two architectural prizes, but continues his study of languages at King's College. Also is writing poetry in his last two years in the city.

1867 Hardy returns to Dorchester in July, working again with John Hicks on ecclesiastical architecture, and turning now to experimenting with fiction.

1868 His first satirical novel *The Poor Man and the Lady* is rejected by two publishers. Hardy is advised by one of the readers, George Meredith, to rewrite or better still put it aside and write another novel. He accepts his advice and starts *Desperate Remedies,* while continuing to write poetry.

1870 In March Hardy journeys to St. Juliot, near Boscastle, Cornwall to draw a plan and take particulars of the church which is to undergo restoration, and there meets Emma Lavinia Gifford, sister-in-law of the Rector. She encourages him to persevere with his writing.

1871 *Desperate Remedies* is published anonymously in March and receives some good notices, but a slating by the *Spectator* reviewer leads to low sales and Hardy suffers a small financial loss.

1872 *Under the Greenwood Tree* (originally titled *The Mellstock Quire*), a happy, humorous book in which Hardy wove first-hand family experiences relating to the church gallery musicians, is published in May, Hardy being paid a small sum for the rights.

1873 *A Pair of Blue Eyes*, set in the corner of North Cornwall he had become familiar with from visiting St. Juliot, is published in May. The book is well received – Tennyson liked it – but the author remains anonymous.

1874 Hardy and Emma are married in London in September. Throughout the year his novel *Far From the Madding Crowd* appears in instalments in *The Cornhill Magazine*, being published in two volumes in November, his name appearing for the first time on a title-page. A success from the first instalment, critics had attributed it to George Eliot.

1876 *The Hand of Ethelberta – A Comedy in Chapters* is published in April, Hardy and Emma having lodged with an invalided captain of smacks and ketches in Swanage the previous autumn and winter while he completed it. A patchwork, it is little acclaimed and constructively criticised. The Hardys make their home at 'Riverside Villa', Sturminster Newton for the next two years, where Hardy writes *The Return of the Native*.

1878 In March the Hardys move to the capital, taking a house just beyond Wandsworth Common. Hardy is elected to the Rabelais Club and finds himself in the company of Browning, Matthew Arnold, Tennyson and others. *The Return of the Native* is published in November.

1880 *The Trumpet-Major*, Hardy's historical romance set in the Napoleonic era which was the precursor to *The Dynasts*, is published in October, pleasing most of the reviewers: 'Mr. Hardy seems to be in the way to do for rural life what Dickens did for that of the town', *Athenaeum*. The day after publication Hardy becomes severely ill with internal haemorrhaging.

1881 Though seriously ill for five months, Hardy completes *A Laodicean – A Story of Today* which 'contained more of the facts of his own life than anything else he had ever written'. When he recovers the Hardys move back to Dorset, to a house in The Avenue, Wimborne.

1882 Hardy's novel *Two on a Tower*, in which he sets 'two infinitesimal lives against the stupendous background of the stellar universe', having appeared serially in the *Atlantic Monthly* is published in the autumn.

1883 The Hardys move to Dorchester in June, living in the county town for the next two years while Max Gate is being built on the outskirts. During this period Hardy writes *The Mayor of Casterbridge*.

1885 Moving into Max Gate in June, they are visited by R. L. Stevenson, then living in Bournemouth – 'I could have got an introduction, but my acquaintance with your mind is already of old date.' Hardy starts work on *The Woodlanders*.

1886 *The Mayor of Casterbridge: The Life and Death of a Man of Character* is published in May. Hardy felt that in the interests of the *Graphic*, where it appeared serially every week, he had been over-inventive, noting: 'I fear it will not be as good as I meant.' But it is well reviewed, Stevenson writing to ask if he might dramatise it. In October William Barnes dies at Winterborne Came rectory, half a mile from Max Gate.

1887 The novel which Hardy later regarded as his best, *The Woodlanders* ('it enabled me to hold my own in fiction, whatever that may be worth.') is published in March. Hardy and Emma spend the Spring travelling in Italy, where the poet takes over from the novelist for a while.

1888 The publication of Hardy's first collection of short stories, *Wessex Tales*.

1891 Having had *Tess of the d'Urbervilles* twice rejected by magazine editors on the grounds of its improper explicitness, Hardy sends hacked version to the *Graphic* who start serialising it in July. Then the uncut novel is published in time for Christmas and has a very mixed press. 'Few would deny the terrible dreariness of this tale.' – *Saturday Review*. 'The new novel is as pitiless and tragic in its intensity as the old Greek dramas.' – *Daily Chronicle*. *A Group of Noble Dames* which also appears during the year draws far less attention.

1894 The publication of Hardy's collection of short stories, *Life's Little Ironies,* which had originally appeared in various magazines. In December the first instalment of *Heart's Insurgent* appears in *Harpers*. As the serialized *Tess* had been, this was a mutilated version of *Jude the Obscure*.

1895 When *Jude the Obscure* 'a novel addressed by a man to men and women of full age' is published in November the onslaught from the press, with a few notable exceptions, is unequalled since the publication of Swinburne's *Poems and Ballards*. Even those who praise are puzzled. 'What has Providence done to Mr. Hardy that he should rise up in the arable land of Wessex and shake his fist at his Creator?' asks Edmund Gosse. It is to be Hardy's last novel. The novelist dies, the poet is reborn.

1897 *The Well-Beloved: A Sketch of a Temperament,* having appeared in serial form in 1892 is published in March, the critics finding little to hammer Hardy about in this rather artificially contrived story with a Portland setting.

1898 In December *Wessex Poems and Other Verses,* Hardy's first collection of poems illustrated with sketches by the writer, is published and generally acclaimed, 'though by some critics not without umbrage at Hardy's having taken the liberty to adopt another vehicle of expression than prose-fiction without consulting them.' *Harper's* advertises them beneath a larger banner for the novels – 'Hundreds of Thousands of these Novels have been sold.' Though most of the poems had been written throughout his years of prose writing, there is a general feeling that he is now trying a new medium of expression, the *Literature* critic preferring the sketches to the poems.

1901 Hardy underlines the fact that he has always been and intends to remain a poet by his choice of title for *Poems of the Past and the Present* when he consolidates his position with their publication in November.

1903 The first part of the work which had been exercising Hardy's mind since at least 1875 – *The Dynasts – An Epic Drama of the War with Napoleon in Three Parts, Nineteen Acts, and One Hundred and Thirty Scenes* is published in December and again greatly confounds his critics; the *Spectator* now charges him with being an incompetent dabbler in philosophic terms.

1904 Jemima Hardy dies in the family cottage at Higher Bockhampton, aged 90, on Easter Day.

1905 In April Aberdeen University bestows his first academic distinction, making Hardy an honorary LL.D.

1906 *The Dynasts* Part II is published in February and is more calmly received. 'Slacken not in winding this glorious poem up to a noble and thrilling conclusion,' wrote Edmund Gosse. 'We can at least acknowledge the magnitude of the conception,' concedes the *Spectator.*

1908 Following publication of *The Dynasts* Part III, the *Spectator:* 'After laying down the last volume admit that we were wrong. Taking the complete poem, we feel that the poet has attained unity, and that the dramatic quality of the whole is his great achievement.'

1909 The third collection of poems, *Time's Laughing-stocks,* is published in December.

1910 In July Hardy is invested by the King with the Order of Merit. He is pleased by the sign of official approval of his work, 'but afterwards I felt that I had failed in the accustomed formalities.' Later in the year he is accorded the freedom of the borough of Dorchester.

1912 Emma Hardy dies on November 27th. Hardy, grief-stricken, travels to Cornwall to arrange the erection of a tablet to her memory in St. Juliot Church. Occasioned by memories of their courtship there forty years before, he writes some of his finest poems. These are later included in the *Poems of 1912–13* section of his *Satires of Circumstance* collection.

1913 Publication of his collection of short stories, *A Changed Man, The Waiting Supper and Other Tales*. 'Why is Mr. Hardy incomparably the greatest of living English novelists?' rhetorically rhapsodises John Baily in *The Bookman*. In June Cambridge University shows its approval by giving him the honorary degree of Doctor of Literature.

1914 On February 10th Hardy is quietly married to Florence Emily Dugdale, a writer of children's stories who had been his secretary for several years. His *Satires of Circumstance* poems are published as World War I begins.

1915 Hardy's elder sister Mary, a talented portrait painter, dies in November and is buried on a cold, wet day 'under the yew tree where the rest of us lie.'

1917 In November *Moments of Vision* is published. Though Hardy wrote: 'I do not expect much notice will be taken of these poems,' the new collection contains some of his finest lyrics, not least amongst them his concluding *Afterwards*.

1920 In February, in the Sheldonian, Jude's creator is made an honorary Doctor of Letters of Oxford University.

1922 Publication in May of *Late Lyrics and Earlier.*

1923 *The Famous Tragedy of the Queen of Cornwall,* based on the Tristan and Iseult legend, is published in November and staged in Dorchester, and later London, by the Hardy Players.

1924 Hardy pays his last respects to Sir Frederick Treves at his funeral on January 2nd. In the *Times* of January 5th appears his *In the Evening,* a poetic tribute to his life-long friend.

1925 *Human Shows, Far Phantasies, Songs and Trifles,* the last collection of poems to appear in Hardy's lifetime, is published.

1928 Hardy dies on January 11th. Pall-bearers at his Westminster Abbey funeral include Baldwin, Ramsay MacDonald, J. M. Barrie, Rudyard Kipling and Bernard Shaw. His heart, removed before cremation, is interred with Emma at Stinsford. Later in the year his final collection of poems, *Winter Words*, which he had prepared for publication on his birthday, is published, the last poem being *He Resolves To Say No More.*

ACKNOWLEDGEMENTS

My thanks are due to Jonathan Cape Ltd. for permission to reprint the quotation accompanying the Frontispiece, and the trustees of the Dorset Natural History & Archaeological Society who gave permission to photograph and reproduce the Turbeville Dames portraits. The Trustees of the Thomas Hardy Memorial Collection in the Dorset County Museum kindly provided the photograph of Thomas Hardy's Study.

I am also gratefully indebted to the following persons and organisations whose ready permission and cheerful co-operation made the compiling of this book such a joyful experience. Admiral R. E. Drax allowed me to photograph the tower in his deer park. The Society for the Protection of Ancient Buildings let me have access to their copy of the *Memories of Church Restoration* MS. Miss E. L. Evans, former curator of Hardy's birthplace, was very helpful and steered me in the direction of the Greenwood Tree. Mr. R. F. Dalton, former curator of the Dorset County Museum, read my first draft and made many useful suggestions and tactful corrections.

In respect to this second edition, I am grateful to my friend Martin Blyth for providing me with a clearer photograph of the Wimborne Minster Quarter Jack, and to Roger Peers and Charles Pettit for pointing out several factual errors in the text of the first edition.

Finally to my wife, Jenny, whose support and encouragement were vital, many thanks for the painstakingly penned maps.

Thomas Hardy's Study, Dorset County Museum

AFTERWARDS

When the Present has latched its postern behind my tremulous stay,
And the May month flaps its glad green leaves like wings,
Delicate-filmed as new-spun silk, will the neighbours say,
"He was a man who used to notice such things"?

If it be in the dusk when, like an eyelid's soundless blink,
The dewfall-hawk comes crossing the shades to alight
Upon the wind-warped upland thorn, a gazer may think,
"To him this must have been a familiar sight."

If I pass during some nocturnal blackness, mothy and warm,
When the hedgehog travels furtively over the lawn,
One may say, "He strove that such innocent creatures should come to no harm,
But he could do little for them; and now he is gone."

If, when hearing that I have been stilled at last, they stand at the door,
Watching the full-starred heavens that winter sees,
Will this thought rise on those who will meet my face no more,
"He was one who had an eye for such mysteries"?

And will any say when my bell of quittance is heard in the gloom,
And a crossing breeze cuts a pause in its outrollings,
Till they rise again, as they were a new bell's boom,
"He hears it not now, but used to notice such things"?

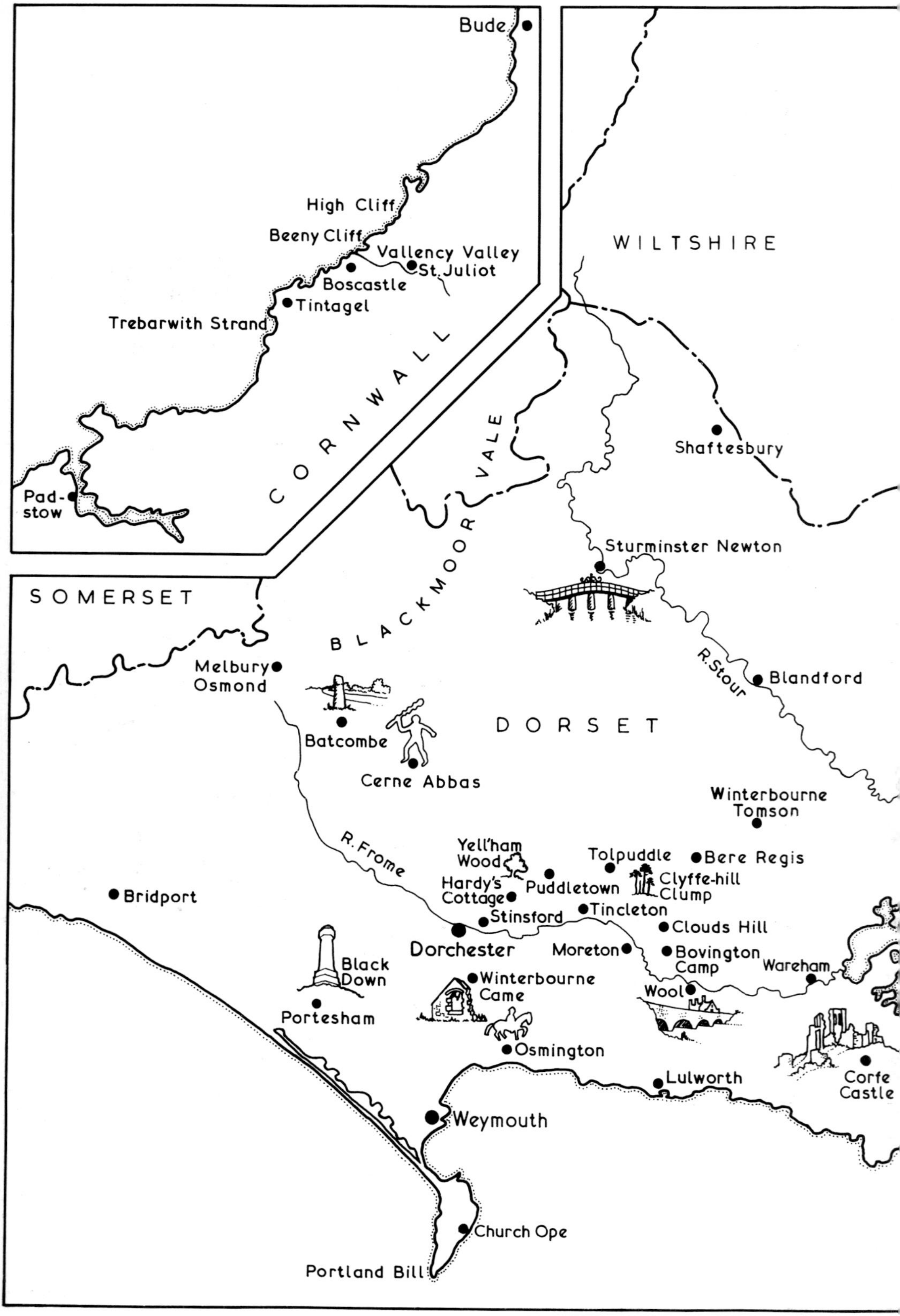
Bude
High Cliff
Beeny Cliff
Vallency Valley
St. Juliot
Boscastle
Tintagel
Trebarwith Strand
CORNWALL
Pad-stow
WILTSHIRE
BLACKMOOR VALE
Shaftesbury
Sturminster Newton
SOMERSET
Melbury Osmond
R. Stour
Blandford
Batcombe
DORSET
Cerne Abbas
Winterbourne Tomson
R. Frome
Yell'ham Wood
Tolpuddle
Bere Regis
Hardy's Cottage
Puddletown
Clyffe-hill Clump
Bridport
Stinsford
Tincleton
Clouds Hill
Dorchester
Moreton
Bovington Camp
Black Down
Wareham
Winterbourne Came
Wool
Portesham
Osmington
Lulworth
Corfe Castle
Weymouth
Church Ope
Portland Bill

LOST AND FOUND

Marilyn Harris is an award-winning, bestselling writer whose work has been translated into many languages. She lives with her family in Oklahoma, USA.

LOST AND FOUND

Marilyn Harris is an award-winning, bestselling writer whose work has been translated into many languages. She lives with her family in Oklahoma, USA.